By Lisa Papademetriou

Based on the television series, "Lizzie McGuire", created by Terri Minsky

New York

Printed in the United States of America

First Edition
3 5 7 9 10 8 6 4

Library of Congress Catalog Card Number: 2004112600

ISBN 0-7868-4634-8
For more Disney Press fun, visit www.disneybooks.com
Visit DisneyChannel.com

CHAPTER ONE

"This is it!" Lizzie McGuire cried as she pressed the volume button on the radio's remote control. "This is the song I was telling you about, Gordo!" She grinned at her best friend David "Gordo" Gordon, who was giving her a dubious look from his place on the McGuires' living room couch.

"I love this band—Simple Sample is so jamtacular!" agreed Lizzie's other best friend, Miranda Sanchez, with a grin.

Lizzie and Miranda joined in as the singer's voice slid into the chorus. "'Where's my little once upon a time?'" they harmonized. "'Seems like dreams are never gonna find . . . me.'"

This is exactly the kind of song I want to write, Lizzie thought as she sang along. And Simple Sample's lead singer, Jyll Hyde, was seriously cool. Lizzie loved her style, her voice—and of course, her rockin' attitude!

Just as Lizzie was getting ready to start in on the second verse, a voice broke in over the music. "Are you a singer-songwriter in the Hillridge area?" the female DJ asked. "If so, you don't want to miss our KZAP songwriting contest—to be judged by Simple Sample!"

"What?" Lizzie screeched, just as Miranda shouted, "Turn it up!"

"You have until Labor Day—that's right, *all* summer—to enter three songs. The winner will receive a recording contract and will perform live onstage with Simple Sample at KZAP's annual End-of-Summer jam. Four runner-ups will get to hear their best song on the *Rich and Jennie Morning Show*!"

Lizzie clicked off the radio. "Miranda, we have to enter!" she cried.

"Of course we're entering," Miranda said. "We've already got a song. We're way ahead of everybody else!"

"Right. Which leads me to my next point—"

Lizzie gave Gordo a meaningful look.

"Just remember, you asked me to be honest," warned Gordo.

Lizzie frowned. Before she'd turned up her favorite song on the radio, she had told Gordo that she wanted his totally objective opinion on her own new song. But now that she was standing in the middle of her living room, about to sing it, she was worried about what he might say.

Miranda folded her arms across her chest. "Just *you* remember, Gordo," she said, "*honest* does not mean *brutal*."

Miranda had been helping Lizzie with her songwriting for the past two weeks. Ever since the final bell rang on the last day of school, they had decided to go full throttle on their "singing careers"—just to see how far they could get. And now, with the KZAP contest, Lizzie thought, we might just get further than we imagined!

Lounging against the sofa pillows, Gordo rolled his eyes. "Okay, okay, I'll be the very embodiment of diplomacy. Now, get this show on the road already."

Lizzie glanced at Miranda. Together they struck a diva pose. "Count it," Lizzie called.

Miranda nodded. "Five, six, seven, eight!"

"'When you're feeling like you want to go for something,'" Lizzie sang.

Miranda leaned toward Lizzie and crooned, "'But that little voice inside your head is holding you back—'"

Then the two girls blended their voices in harmony. "'There's no need to be blue. I've got three words for you. You go, girl!'"

Lizzie and Miranda moved through the opening steps of Miranda's slick, hip-hop choreography. Lizzie thought they were getting seriously tight, which was good news, especially since the winner of the KZAP contest would have to perform live onstage!

How could we not enter?
We've got the song.
we've got the moves. . . .

Just then, Lizzie tripped on the edge of the carpet and flailed madly, cartwheeling toward the coffee table.

Okay, we've got the song.

Note to self, Lizzie thought as she quickly recovered, roll up the carpet before our next rehearsal.

Working her way back into synch with Miranda, Lizzie smiled at their audience of one and caught up in time to hit the chorus:

"Yeah, you go, girl!
You've got the skills—
Take a risk, use your power.
You're the woman of the hour.
You go, girl!

You've got the will—
You can do it, you can make it,
And you've got no need to fake it.
Believe what I am saying—
You've got it,
Now use it—
Girl!"

Breathing hard, Lizzie and Miranda hit their final pose with a grin.

"Well, what do you think?" Lizzie asked as she and Miranda straightened up.

Gordo blinked at her from the couch. "I think I'm really getting in touch with my feminine power," he said dryly.

"Gordo!" Lizzie and Miranda chorused.

"No, no, it was great," Gordo said. "You guys really seemed like you were having fun."

"'Having fun'?" Miranda repeated, her dark eyes narrowing. "Gordo, that's what people say when you stink."

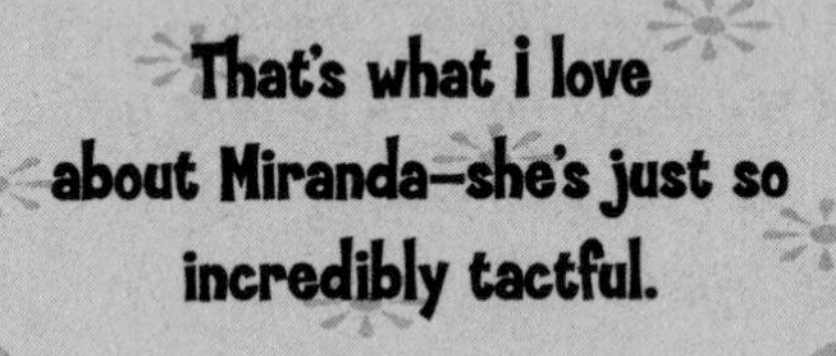

"I didn't mean it that way," Gordo insisted, shoving his mop of curly brown hair out of his blue eyes. "The song is really great. It's just that—I think it would be better if it had a strong backbeat behind it."

"I knew it!" Miranda said, throwing up her hands in frustration. "The song doesn't work without music."

"But what about the moves?" Lizzie asked. "Don't they help you get a sense of the rhythm?" That'll be important when we perform at the End-of-Summer jam, Lizzie thought.

Gordo shoved his floppy hair out of his

eyes again. "You were doing dance moves?" he asked.

"Gordo, I think it's time for a haircut," Miranda said.

"Look, it's a radio contest," Gordo pointed out. "It's cool that you have choreography, but the most important thing is the song."

Lizzie sighed. She knew her friends were right—but she wasn't sure what to do about it. "Could we get some kind of percussion machine?" Lizzie suggested.

"Lizzie, if we're going to win that contest, we need more than some generic karaoke device backing us up," Miranda pointed out.

"Well, you could go to a recording studio and cut a demo CD," Gordo suggested. "They have professional musicians who'll record with you."

"Great idea, Gordo," Lizzie said, flopping onto the couch beside her friend. "Now all we have to do is find a recording studio that will help us out for *free*."

"Well . . ." Miranda perched on the edge of the couch on the other side of Gordo. "I've got fifty dollars."

Lizzie lifted one eyebrow suspiciously at her friend. "Where did you get fifty dollars?" she asked, tucking her legs beneath her. She was wearing a comfy orange velour workout suit, her hair tied back with a sparkly orange bandana. Style meets workout, Lizzie had thought when she put it together.

"I've been selling my parents' old records on eBay," Miranda confessed.

"Hmm." Gordo fiddled with a couch pillow. "You've been spending a lot of time online lately."

"Hey!" Miranda said defensively. "Some of those Captain and Tennille records are worth serious *dinero*."

"Okay, so fifty bucks is a start," Lizzie said, "but we're still going to need to get more cash from somewhere." She and Miranda turned to Gordo.

"Hey, don't look at me!" Gordo said, holding up his hands. "I'm completely broke. I can't even afford a haircut."

"Oh, come on, Gordo," Lizzie said, giving him a nudge. "You know you hoard your allowance like a squirrel hoards nuts."

"Yeah, Gordo," Miranda agreed. "Admit it."

"Okay, usually that's true," Gordo confessed. "But I just signed up for a summer film class at the community center. It costs two hundred dollars—and now I'm flat busted."

Lizzie let out a groan. There *has* to be a way to get that money, she thought.

"Hey, I have an idea," Gordo announced.

Ooh, I love having a genius as one of my best friends! Lizzie thought. Gordo always comes through with a plan. "What? What?" she asked eagerly.

"Let's eat something," Gordo said.

"Gordo!" Lizzie and Miranda moaned.

"What?" Gordo said. "I'm hungry. And I can't think on an empty stomach."

"Fine," Lizzie said, hopping off the couch. "Let's hit the Digital Bean." The Digital Bean was their favorite cybercafé—and it had the world's best muffins and smoothies. "We can surf the Web and see how much money we're going to need to record our song."

"And maybe we'll come up with a way to raise the cash," Miranda suggested as she followed Lizzie out the front door.

Thud!

Lizzie and Miranda turned to see Gordo frowning at the doorframe and rubbing his head. "Where did that come from?" he asked, brushing his long brown curls out of his face.

"It really *is* time for a haircut, Gordo," Miranda told him.

"Hi, Mom!" Lizzie said brightly as she walked into the kitchen later that day.

"Hi, honey." Mrs. McGuire didn't look up. She was staring intently at a tiny pine tree, her scissors hovering above a branch.

Lizzie sat down beside her mom at the kitchen table. "What are you doing?"

"Bonsai," Mrs. McGuire said. "It's a Japanese art form. You're supposed to trim back the branches so that it looks like an ancient full-size tree, only tinier. But I can't decide where to cut."

Leave it to my mom to come up with the world's weirdest hobby. Next to my dad's, of course.

Lizzie could just picture her dad's collection of garden gnomes being shaded by her mother's miniature forest of munchkin trees.

Sheesh. How in the world did i turn out normal?

"So, Mom," Lizzie said carefully, "I need to talk to you about something."

After three hours of research at the Digital Bean, she and Miranda had discovered three things: first, a studio session to cut their demo would cost three hundred dollars. Second, after smoothies, muffins, and computer time, they were now nine dollars and fifty cents poorer than they had been when they started. Third, there was no way around it—they were going to have to ask their parents for money.

Mrs. McGuire peered at her daughter over the top of her black-rimmed glasses.

Lizzie cleared her throat. "Did I mention that your hair looks . . . really great today?"

"How much is that compliment going to cost me?" Mrs. McGuire asked.

Is she reading my mind? Lizzie wondered.

"Three hundred dollars?" Lizzie weakly asked her mother.

Mrs. McGuire's eyes got big. "Three hundred dollars?" she repeated in her *Are-you-insane?* voice.

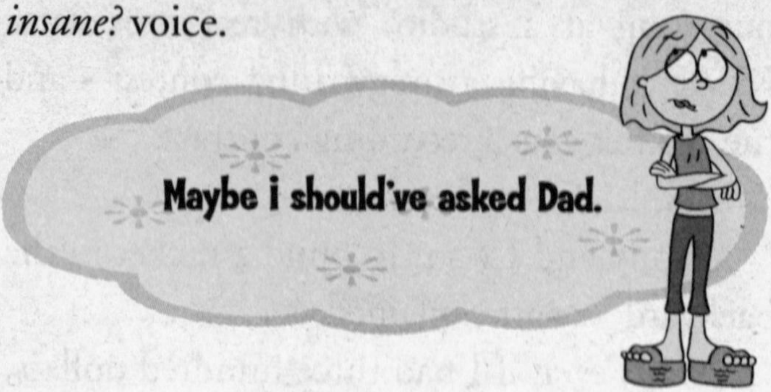

Maybe i should've asked Dad.

"I swear I'll pay you back," Lizzie said quickly. Once we win that KZAP contest, we'll have plenty of money, Lizzie thought.

"Hey, Mom." Lizzie's annoying little brother, Matt, picked that moment to walk into the kitchen. "Can I have three hundred dollars?"

Mrs. McGuire put down her shears. "Why does everybody need three hundred dollars?" she asked in frustration.

"I don't know why the rodent needs money," Lizzie said, flashing her brother an evil look, "but Miranda and I want to record our song at a studio, with real musicians. KZAP is having a songwriting contest—and the winner gets a recording contract."

Mrs. McGuire frowned.

"Lanny and I want to build a rocket in the backyard," Matt explained.

"Matt, even if I had three hundred dollars, I wouldn't let you build a rocket in the backyard," Mrs. McGuire informed him.

"But it's educational!" Matt wailed.

"Mom, please," Lizzie begged, ignoring her little brother. "This is really important."

Mrs. McGuire sighed. "Sweetheart, it's a lot of money," she said, shaking her head.

"But you've heard the song," Lizzie protested. "We can win the contest, Mom."

"I think the song is great," Mrs. McGuire agreed. "But I just don't have three hundred dollars to give you, honey. I'm sorry. Maybe you could earn it by doing a little babysitting around the neighborhood," she suggested. "You could start by looking after Matt sometimes."

Babysitting . . . Lizzie thought. It wasn't a bad idea. . . .

"Yeah, right." Matt rolled his eyes.

Suddenly, Lizzie's brain was flooded with images of the times she'd taken care of Matt and his friend Lanny. There was the time

Lanny had gotten his head stuck in the toilet. There was the time Matt and Lanny had busted her dad's prized football and then disappeared, looking for a way to fix it. There was the time Matt had decided to hold a scavenger hunt, and had hidden lunch meat all over the house for Lanny to find. Unfortunately, Lanny hadn't found all of it, and the McGuires spent the next five months finding moldy, stinky slices of baloney in places where they least expected.

Okay, so babysitting is a no-go. Maybe I'll try something else, Lizzie thought. *But Mom does have a point. I could get some kind of job.* Of course, she'd once worked as a busboy at the Digital Bean, and that had been a certifiable disaster. Her ex–best friend, Kate Sanders, and Kate's lackey Claire Miller had come in every day to torture Lizzie on the job. *I'll just have to find something better,*

Lizzie decided. Maybe something involving fashion!

Mrs. McGuire snipped at a branch on her bonsai. "Oh, shoot!" she cried as a tiny branch fell onto the table. "I didn't mean to do that." She put down the scissors in frustration.

Matt picked up the little container that held the tiny tree, and turned it one way, then another. Putting it down, he looked at the shears. "May I?" he asked his mom.

She waved her hands at him, surrendering. "It's all yours. I give up."

Matt made a few snips in the air with the scissors, then attacked the bonsai. *Snip! Snip!*

A moment later, Matt stood back proudly. "There you go."

"Wow," Mrs. McGuire said, her eyebrows lifted in surprise. "That looks—great."

Lizzie gaped at the tiny tree. It had gone

from looking like a scraggly little weed to looking like an ancient, proud pine tree . . . all with a few cuts from Matt.

Matt grinned smugly. "Can I have it?" he asked, holding up the bonsai.

"It's all yours," Mrs. McGuire told him.

"Excellent," Matt said. "I've been meaning to work on my scissor skills."

Lizzie rolled her eyes. I don't even want to know what that means, she thought. Hauling herself out of the chair, Lizzie trudged toward the stairs. She had to call Miranda and figure out possible jobs.

Hey, Lizzie thought, where there's a will, there's a way.

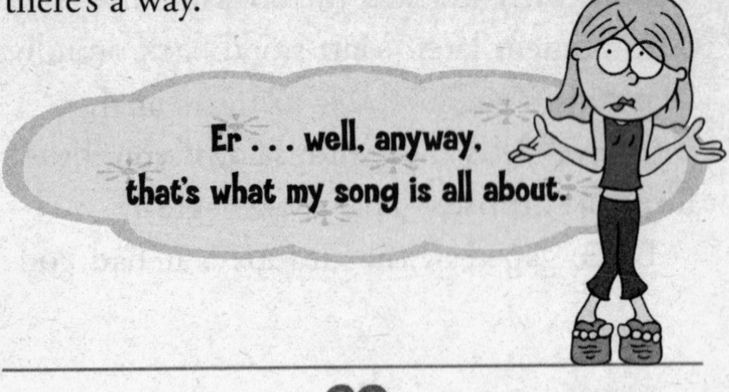

Er . . . well, anyway, that's what my song is all about.

CHAPTER TWO

"I spent the morning cruising the mall," Miranda griped as she lay back on her lounge chair and adjusted her pink-rimmed sunglasses. "All of the good jobs are taken."

"What about the not-so-good jobs?" Gordo asked.

"Gordo, I am not selling shoes at the Toe Barn," Miranda snapped. "Do you know what foot dandruff is? No thanks."

"What we need is a job *here*," Lizzie said,

looking around the community pool. It was a gorgeous summer day—hot but with a light breeze. The sky was a brilliant blue, the pool was clean and cool, and tons of cute guys in swim trunks were chilling out in the shallow end. "It would be great if we could just hang here all day, every day."

"Not for me," Gordo said, adjusting his bowling shirt and baseball cap. "I burn too easily."

Lizzie sighed. Gordo was the only person in the world who would wear a vintage shirt to the pool. The guy definitely had his own style. Or antistyle, depending on how you wanted to look at it.

Miranda rolled her eyes. "Have you ever heard of something called sunblock?"

"Sunblock is for people who spend time outside," Gordo pointed out, "doing sporty things. I'm more of an indoorsman. Actually,

I'm already too hot." He stood up. "Anybody want a smoothie?"

"You could just cool off in the pool," Miranda suggested.

"Perhaps you didn't hear me right," Gordo replied. "*Indoorsman.* So—smoothies?"

"We'll come with you," Lizzie said. She and Miranda extricated themselves from the plastic-slatted lounge chairs, and the three friends headed toward the snack bar.

"Hi, what can I get for you?" asked the guy behind the counter. He had a superwide smile and a round face. He was kind of cute, Lizzie thought, even though he was wearing a dorky orange shirt and a cap that said HILLRIDGE COMMUNITY POOL in green block letters. His orange name tag read SCOTT.

Miranda scanned the smoothie list. "So many choices . . ."

Scott glanced at the list, then turned back

to Miranda. "I recommend the raspberry-kiwi." His dark eyes twinkled. "My specialty."

"Okay," Miranda said playfully, "but I expect it to be special."

"Make it two," Lizzie put in.

"And a banana-strawberry," Gordo added.

"Coming right up." Scott hauled some fruit out and put it in the blender along with some yogurt and ice.

"I'll be right back," Gordo said as Scott started blending the first drink. "The list of supplies for my film class is supposed to be on the bulletin board." The community center where he was going to be taking the film class was right next door.

Lizzie leaned against the snack bar and watched the pool as Gordo left. The chiseled, blond lifeguard was lounging in his tall chair, looking ultracool with his mirrored shades. He lazily twirled his whistle around his finger.

"Now, that's the perfect summer job," Lizzie said with a sigh.

"Tell me about it," Miranda said, shoving her sunglasses on top of her head. "The hardest thing about it is tooting your whistle at the kids splashing in the shallow end. The rest is all suntans and getting paid to chill at the pool. Not to mention hanging with the hottie guy lifeguards," Miranda added, waggling her eyebrows up and down.

"Too bad we aren't old enough to lifeguard," Lizzie said. "I hear it pays really well, too."

"'Seems like dreams are never gonna find . . . me,'" Miranda sang softly, quoting the Simple Sample song.

Lizzie sighed.

Just then, Scott plunked their raspberry-kiwi smoothies on the counter. "Why don't you take the junior lifeguarding classes?" he suggested.

"What?" Lizzie asked.

"The junior lifeguarding classes," Scott said, gesturing toward the bulletin board. "It's a two-week course, and the person with the top score in the class gets the assistant lifeguard position for the rest of the summer. I think it pays eight dollars and fifty cents an hour. You'd be helping out Tate." He nodded at the gorgeous lifeguard perched on the tall chair.

Lizzie's eyebrows flew up. *Whoa.* Cash money to work at the pool with Mr. Hottie? she thought. Sign me up! Her crush, Ethan Craft, was away at camp for the summer—so Lizzie had been seriously cuteness-deprived.

"How much does the class cost?" Miranda asked.

"It's free," Scott explained. "It's considered a community service, since you learn CPR and all that stuff."

"That's our price!" Miranda said, grinning at Lizzie.

Recording studio, here we come! Lizzie thought. "Let's go put our names down."

"Thanks so much," Miranda told Scott, as she picked up both her smoothie and Gordo's.

Scott smiled. "What's your name, by the way?" he asked.

"Miranda. And this is Lizzie." Miranda took a sip of her smoothie.

"Hi," Lizzie said.

"Well, if you're taking the lifeguarding class, I guess I'll be seeing a lot of you." His cheeks dimpled as his smile grew wider. "Lucky me."

"Lucky us," Miranda said, holding up her smoothie. "This is awesome!"

Scott shrugged. "I told you they were my specialty."

Wow, Lizzie thought as she took a sip of the drink, Miranda is right. It's sweet and tart at the same time—delicious. I'm so glad Gordo wanted a smoothie. This has been our lucky day!

And there was something else Lizzie had noticed. "Is it just my imagination," she asked Miranda as they headed toward Gordo, "or was Smoothie Scott doing a lot of smiling in your direction?"

"What can I say?" Miranda asked, flipping her shades down over her eyes and grinning slyly. "When you've got it, you've got it."

Lizzie laughed.

The girls found Gordo scanning the bulletin board for the list of supplies for his course.

"Look, we'll be the first names on the junior-lifeguard class list," Miranda said. She picked up the pen that was dangling from a string attached to the bulletin board and wrote down her name.

Lizzie added her name below Miranda's.

"Why would I have to bring an unlined sketchbook with a *black* cover to the class?" Gordo asked no one in particular.

"Maybe so you can sketch out ideas for scenes?" Lizzie suggested.

Gordo looked up. "But why a black cover?"

"Because black coordinates with everything?" Miranda volunteered.

Gordo rolled his eyes. "That's ridiculous. But I guess there has to be a good reason." He looked over at the flyer announcing the junior lifeguarding classes. "Hey, cool," Gordo said.

"And the best person in the class gets to be the assistant lifeguard," Lizzie explained. "It pays."

"Well, it looks like one of you will get the

job," Gordo said. "Considering that you're the only two people on the list."

"Jamtacular," Lizzie said, "because we need the money."

"Listen, Lizzie, if you get the job, I'll be here every day helping you out," Miranda volunteered. "That way, it'll be like we're earning the money together."

"Same," Lizzie said with a smile. "But classes don't start for another week," she pointed out. "I'm sure we'll have some competition."

Yeah . . . and if we're lucky, that competition will look gorgeous in swim trunks!

Gordo walked into the classroom at the

community center the following afternoon and stopped in his tracks. For a second, he was worried that he had wandered into a funeral. Everyone was dressed in black. He checked the information sheet in his hand, then looked at his watch. No—he had the right place, right day, right time. Besides, everybody had little black sketchbooks perched on their laps. . . .

"Don't panic," whispered a voice behind him. "It's not a funeral."

Turning, Gordo saw a heavyset girl in a vintage yellow-flowered dress sitting in an aisle seat toward the rear. She had straight black hair in a strange, severe Cleopatra cut, and wore totally unfashionable glasses with rims as red as her lipstick. The journal in her lap was red, too. "At least, I hope it isn't," she added. "But I'm sitting in the back, so I can make a quick exit, just in case."

"Good idea," Gordo said, taking a seat beside the girl. "I'm Gordo."

"Lucy." She frowned at him. "But you aren't fat."

"What?" Gordo asked.

"*Gordo* means 'fatso' in Spanish," Lucy explained. "Didn't you know that?"

"It's short for Gordon—my last name," Gordo explained, but he was thinking that it was mighty interesting that Miranda had never mentioned that his nickname was a major insult in Spanish. He was going to have to remember to ask her about that later. Picking up his video camera, Gordo hit the ON switch and panned across the backs of the black-clad students at the front of the class. A few of them wore sunglasses, and one guy was even sporting a beret. "Film class, day one," he narrated. "Most of the students seem to think that they are either in Hollywood or Paris."

Lucy laughed. "Maybe we'll be filming in black-and-white," she suggested.

One of the students took a delicate sip from a paper coffee cup.

"Notice the tools of the trade," Gordo whispered, his camera rolling. "The take-out coffeehouse beverage, the laid-back chair slouch, the sunglasses . . ."

"The hair gel," Lucy added.

Just then, the teacher walked in. He was a tall, lanky guy with a shaved head and an earring. He wore black pants and a black T-shirt.

"Apparently, I missed some kind of dress code memo," Gordo said, looking down at his khaki shorts and vintage shirt.

Lucy cocked an eyebrow. "I guess neither one of us is on the right mailing list."

"My name is Hathaway von Zellsburg, but I urge you all to call me Hathaway," the smooth-headed teacher said in a clipped voice. "This is a five-week course, designed to bring out the best in your creative selves. We will be watching films, reading scripts, and discussing how to set up individual shots—all of which will culminate in a final short film on the subject of your choice. You can choose either documentary or traditional narrative—I don't believe in artistic boundaries."

Lucy scribbled something in her notebook and held it out for Gordo to see. *Is that British accent for real?* the note said.

Gordo grinned and shook his head. He thought Hathaway's accent sounded about as real as his first name.

"The best film at the end of our five weeks together will be entered in the Hillridge Student Film Festival," Hathaway explained. "The runner-up will receive Honorable Mention."

"Um, excuse me?" Gordo asked, raising his hand.

Hathaway eyed him coolly. "Yes?"

"I was just wondering—why did we have to bring an unlined journal with a black cover?" Gordo asked.

"To make notes and sketch out scenes," Hathaway said. "And black coordinates with everything."

Lucy let out a snort.

"In a few moments, I will show you a classic film by the Japanese director Kurosawa," Hathaway went on. The other students bent over their little black notebooks, scribbling madly. "It's called *Rashomon.* Notice the interplay of light and shadow."

Lucy leaned toward Gordo as Hathaway turned off the overhead lights and pressed PLAY on the VCR. "I love Kurosawa," Lucy whispered.

Gordo nodded. "This movie is one of my favorites. I've already seen it twice."

A wry smile ticked up in the corner of Lucy's mouth. "Seven times."

Gordo lifted his eyebrows. *Seven?* He couldn't even persuade Lizzie and Miranda to watch it once. They said the subtitles gave them a headache.

"I love Japanese films," Lucy explained. "And Hong Kong martial-arts movies, too. I'm thinking maybe I'll update part of *The Seven Samurai* for my project—put in lots of fight scenes." Her black eyes twinkled behind her big, red-rimmed glasses. "What about you—any ideas?"

"I don't know. . . ." Gordo admitted. He glanced around the classroom at the small clusters of black-clad artistes who were gazing up at Hathaway as though his bald head held the answers to the film universe. Gordo would have bet anything that most of the films from the students in that class would come out the same. They'd probably all be just like *Rashomon*, in fact. Gordo sighed as he watched the opening credits roll, thinking that it was ridiculous how people would rather copy a good idea than come up with one of their own. At that moment, a plan started to take shape in Gordo's head. "I think I might do something about nerds," he said slowly.

"Nerds?" Lucy repeated.

"Sure—" Gordo spoke faster as the idea started to come together, "a documentary about what separates them from the so-called cool kids."

"You mean like five rows of folding chairs?" Lucy suggested, eyeing the empty rows between them and the Legion of Darkness.

"Something like that," Gordo admitted. "I'm not sure yet."

"Groovy." Lucy grinned. "I'm available for interviews."

"You two in the back row," Hathaway called from the front of the class. "Please pay attention to the film. You can learn a lot from Kurosawa."

A few of the vampires at the front turned around and scowled at Lucy and Gordo.

Gordo smiled at Lucy, who rolled her eyes, then they both sat back to watch the film. But Gordo couldn't focus very well—he kept thinking about his project. He realized that the film class itself would make a perfect documentary.

He just needed to figure out the right spin.

CHAPTER THREE

"Which do you like?" Lizzie asked as she held up two bikinis for her friends' inspection. One was green with fuchsia and purple stripes, and the other was solid blue.

"Hmm." Miranda sat at Lizzie's computer, frowning at the choices. "What happened to the pink polka-dotted one?"

"It digs at my waist," said Lizzie.

"What about the yellow flowered one?" Miranda suggested.

"I can't find it," Lizzie admitted. "But do you think it's better? Maybe I should try looking for it again."

"May I just ask why you're wearing a bikini to a junior lifeguarding class?" Gordo interrupted.

Can Gordo be any more clueless?
The boy is *so* fashion impaired.

"I'm wearing a bikini because it's the first day, and I want to make a good impression," Lizzie told Gordo.

"And because the head lifeguard is a major hottie," Miranda added. "Go for the blue."

"Really?" Lizzie said, frowning at the blue bikini. "I hate the shoulder straps."

Miranda shrugged. "Then go for the stripe."

"Doesn't it make me look like a beach umbrella?" Lizzie asked.

"Make it stop. Make it stop!" Gordo groaned.

Lizzie tossed both bikinis on her bed. "Oh, forget it," she said. "I'm going to look for the yellow bikini." She knew that Gordo had a seriously low tolerance for girl talk. *I'll spare him,* she decided.

Miranda turned back to the computer as Lizzie dug through her drawers. She unearthed her green one-piece and her goggles, but the yellow bikini was nowhere to be found. *Where are you, yellow swimsuit?* Lizzie wondered, looking around her room.

Suddenly, a dim memory flashed through her mind . . . she had thrown the bikini in the back of her closet after her family went to the beach last Labor Day. Lizzie knelt down and started to search the bottom of the closet.

"You've got mail," Lizzie's computer chirped as Miranda clicked on an icon.

"Any word from Mystery Guy?" Lizzie asked.

Miranda couldn't hide a smile as she double-clicked. "Yep."

Gordo looked up from the movie magazine he was reading. "Who?"

"Miranda's been exchanging e-mails with this guy she met online," Lizzie explained.

Gordo lifted his eyebrows.

"It's not as weird as it sounds," Miranda said defensively. "I met him in Hillridge Chat Central."

HCC was a closed chat room for kids who went to middle schools in the Hillridge Independent School District. Anyone with a student ID number from Hillridge Junior

High, Central Middle School, or Twin Groves could log on. The chat room was screened and monitored, too, so it was safe.

"It's not creepy or anything. We just talk about the kind of music we like and stuff. He doesn't even know my last name."

"You hope," Gordo said.

"What does he say?" Lizzie asked, ignoring Gordo.

" 'Hey, Chilipeppa17,' " Miranda read, " 'just finished listening to the latest CD by Tea Time for Johnny, and you're right—they rock. Well, what I could hear of them rocked. My little sister is learning to play the trumpet, and her room is right next to mine. She isn't any good, but she's definitely loud. Let me know how your first day of lifeguard class goes. I know you'll make a big splash. (I know, I know—*groan.*) Waterboy335.' " Miranda turned to her friends, grinning.

"He's funny," Gordo admitted. "Then again, a lot of creeps have a great sense of humor."

"Gordo!" Lizzie snapped. She turned to Miranda, still feeling around on the bottom of her closet for the lost bikini. "He sounds really cool." Suddenly, Lizzie's hand closed around a piece of fabric. "Gotcha!" she shouted, pulling up the bottom half of the yellow bikini. Lizzie frowned. "Where's the rest of you?" Tossing aside the half of her bikini, Lizzie sat down on the floor and groaned in frustration.

Miranda gave her friend a sympathetic look. "Mall?" she suggested.

"Is there any other way?" Lizzie asked. She was pretty sure she could convince her parents to spring for a new bathing suit—since she was going to learn to save lives, and all that junk.

"You have four swimsuits!" Gordo cried.

"Yes, but none of them are the *right* swimsuit," Miranda pointed out. "So Lizzie might as well have none."

Gordo threw up his hands. "All that matters is that you have a swimsuit. It's a lifeguard class, not a beauty contest."

"I care about how I look," Lizzie shot back. "Is that such a crime?"

"With that hair you can't even *see* the bathing suits," Miranda pointed out, eyeing the floppy mop of curly hair still hanging in his eyes. "So you really shouldn't be handing out fashion advice, Gordo."

"Fine," Gordo said. "Go to the mall. But I'm not coming with you. And by the way, Miranda"—Gordo's voice took on a suspicious tone—"someone just told me that my name means 'fatso,' in Spanish. Care to comment?"

"What?" Lizzie cried, gaping at Miranda.

Miranda's face flushed bright red.

"You knew!" Gordo cried. "No wonder all of your relatives cracked up when you introduced me to them last Thanksgiving!"

"Gordo, I didn't mean to embarrass you, I swear," Miranda insisted.

Gordo slapped his magazine down on the bed. "Then why didn't you tell me?"

Miranda winced. "Gordo, do you remember when we met?"

"Second grade," Gordo said, scowling.

"And you were going through that phase—" Miranda prompted.

"The three-Twinkies-a-day phase!" Lizzie blurted, remembering. At school, Gordo had been known as the Twinkie Kid.

"Well," Miranda hesitated, "you were kind of . . ."

"Round?" Gordo finished for her.

Miranda nodded. "Yeah. And I didn't want to hurt your feelings. Then, I guess, you stopped eating all those Twinkies, and once you weren't so round, your nickname didn't seem like a big deal anymore—"

"Okay," Gordo said finally. "Just don't let me go on any more Spanish game shows with that nickname. It's embarrassing."

"Cross my heart," Miranda promised.

"Knock, knock," Matt announced as he and his silent friend Lanny walked right into Lizzie's room.

"Matt, why don't you actually *knock*, instead of just saying 'knock, knock' and barging in *uninvited*?" Lizzie demanded.

Matt shrugged. "Because you might not let me in. This way, you have no choice."

Lanny nodded.

"He has a point," Gordo admitted.

"Lanny and I were wondering if any of you needed a haircut," Matt announced.

"Gordo does," Miranda said.

"We're only charging seven bucks," Matt said. Lanny gave him a pointed look. Matt nodded and added, "*Five* for friends and family."

Lizzie shook her head. "Matt, do you think we're completely cra—"

"Okay," Gordo said.

"What?" Lizzie gaped at him. "Are you seriously considering letting my pineapple-headed brother cut your hair?"

Gordo shrugged. "Why not? It's only five bucks."

"You won't be sorry," Matt said. "I've been practicing on my bonsai."

"I can't watch this," Lizzie announced, covering her eyes.

"The horror," Miranda agreed, shaking her

head. "Gordo, I knew you weren't into fashion, but this . . ." She struggled for words and came up blank.

"We'll be at the mall," Lizzie said. "Gordo, I beg you. Get out while you still can."

"It'll be fine," Gordo said, hopping off Lizzie's bed.

"Step into my office," Matt said, rubbing his hands together. Lanny gestured for Gordo to follow, and the two little boys exited Lizzie's room.

Gordo started to follow—then walked face-first into Lizzie's doorframe. "I meant to do that," he said, rubbing his forehead.

Miranda and Lizzie exchanged looks. "Well, he really does need a haircut," Miranda noted.

"Yeah," Lizzie agreed, "and it's too bad the first thing he'll see is what Matt has done to his hair."

* * *

Gordo shoved his floppy brown bangs out of his eyes as he walked into the bedroom next to Lizzie's. Matt had taken the mirror down from behind his dresser and propped it up on his desk. There were newspapers on the floor around the desk chair.

"Have a seat," Matt said, gesturing to the chair.

Gordo sat down, and Lanny wrapped a towel around his neck. Spotting Matt's bonsai on the desk, Gordo tried to comfort himself with the fact that the tiny tree really did look very good—nicely trimmed.

"I just want the same haircut that I have now," Gordo told Matt. "Only about an inch and a half shorter."

Matt looked at him in the mirror, then picked up one of Gordo's curls and let it drop. He squinted at Gordo's hair. "Hmm," he said. "Have you considered layers?"

"No layers."

"You could do something structural. . . ." Matt went on. "I'm thinking pinecone—"

"No pinecones," Gordo repeated, "I just want a regular haircut. The *same* haircut."

"Same haircut, okay," Matt said absent-mindedly. He grabbed a pair of what looked like gardening shears and made a few experimental snips in the air. "Lanny?"

Lanny, who was standing by Matt's boom box, popped in a CD and pressed PLAY. A moment later, the opening strains of Beethoven's Fifth Symphony blasted through the room.

With a deep breath, Matt closed his eyes and held up his hands as the music washed over him.

Gordo was starting to suspect that Lizzie may have been right about trusting Matt with a haircut. Bad idea. "What are you doing?" he finally asked as a little wave of nervousness overtook his stomach.

Matt opened his eyes. "Waiting for my inspiration." He closed his eyes again.

Gordo was just reassuring himself that Matt would open his eyes any minute when Lizzie's brother reached out and grabbed a hunk of Gordo's hair, and then—without looking—hacked away at it, and another hunk in the back.

"Whoa!" Gordo shouted, but Matt kept snipping. The brown curls fluttered to the floor as Gordo stared at Matt in shock. He was slashing at Gordo's head with the shears, hacking off clump after clump of hair, which began to pile up on the newspapers like autumn leaves. His snips were timed to the music, and Matt cut and cut, eyes closed, his fingers feeling the hair with one hand, chopping away with the other.

Lanny clapped excitedly.

Gordo told himself to move, to get out of the chair, to get away at all costs—but he was frozen in shock. It was too late, anyway. Matt was on a roll. There was no stopping him now.

CHAPTER FOUR

"Okay, lip-gloss check," Lizzie said as she and Miranda walked out of the changing room at the community pool the next day.

"Unsmeared," Miranda confirmed. "Mine?"

"Jamtacular," Lizzie said. She smiled, looking down at the purple-and-green-swirl bathing suit she had on. Lizzie had decided to take Gordo's advice and go for a one-piece, after all, and she and Miranda had both found totally cute ones on sale at the mall.

Okay, sure, the hottie lifeguard is way older and not likely to pay much attention to a junior high school girl, but still . . . when one is near cuteness, one wants to look her best!

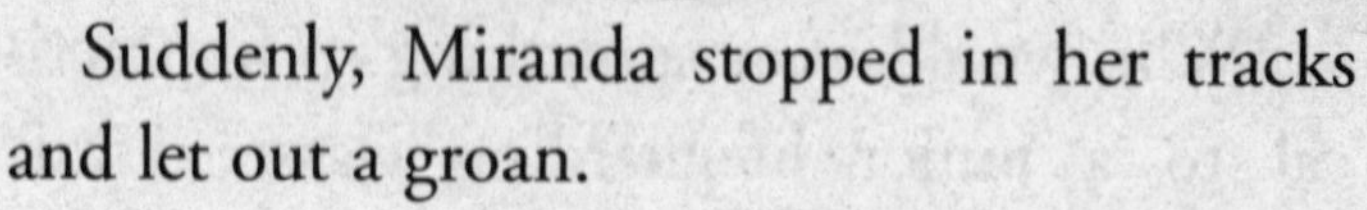

Suddenly, Miranda stopped in her tracks and let out a groan.

"What?" Lizzie asked, looking toward the edge of the pool, where Miranda was staring. "Oh, no."

"Oh, yes," Miranda said.

There were five kids gathered at the edge of the pool for their junior lifeguarding class, and front and center was a girl with a mass of blond curls in a hot-pink bikini. It was Kate Sanders, Lizzie's former friend and current pain in the rear. Kate was queen of the school, and basically lived to make Lizzie feel like an idiot. Standing beside Kate was her snobby, she-beast lackey, Claire Miller.

Lizzie felt her dreams of leisurely lifeguarding disappearing down the pool drain. *Kate!* Lizzie thought. *What could be worse?* She gritted her teeth, eyeing Kate's glamorous bikini.

"Who would wear something so impractical to a junior lifeguarding class?" Lizzie angrily hissed to Miranda.

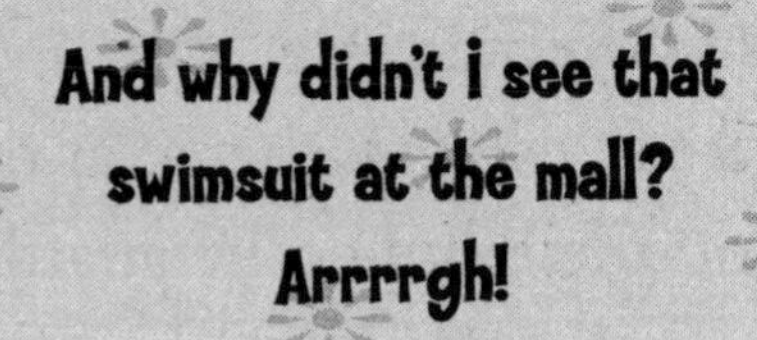

Kate narrowed her eyes at Lizzie as she and Miranda joined the other kids at the side of the pool. Kate whispered something to Claire, who giggled.

"Something funny?" Miranda asked, raising her eyebrows so high they disappeared into her straight black bangs.

Kate tossed her long blond hair. "Nothing," she said easily. "I was just telling Claire that I couldn't wait to see Lizzie flop in the pool."

"I can swim," Lizzie said defensively.

"Right," Kate said, rolling her eyes. "You can hardly walk down the hall without falling flat on your face."

That is so not true! it's those open locker doors i have a problem with . . . and those stupid garbage cans that are always tripping me. But that's all!

Kate grinned evilly, and Lizzie felt her cheeks burn. "I hope you aren't counting on getting the top slot in the class, Lizzie," she went on.

"Kate's going to be the assistant lifeguard," Claire announced smugly.

Kate gave Lizzie a tight little smile and said, "So you can give it up."

"We're not giving anything up," Miranda snapped. "You two can eat our bubbles."

Lizzie smiled. That was one of the many things she liked best about Miranda—Kate didn't scare her one bit.

Kate folded her arms across her chest. She glared at Miranda and warned, "That job is mine."

"Kate's using the money to get a complete makeover at Dominic Dunay Salon," Claire bragged, naming the fanciest day spa in Hillridge.

Please tell me they're going to make over her personality, too.

Kate studied her manicure. "That way, I'll look even better when we start school in the fall. And you two," she said, pointing a French tip at Lizzie, "will be completely invisible. As usual."

"Get that finger out of my friend's face," Miranda threatened. "The only thing that's about to get made over is your attitude when Lizzie smokes you."

Okay, thought Lizzie uneasily, now Miranda is going a little too far. I'm not *that* good. "All right, all right, Miranda," Lizzie murmured. "I think she gets the point."

"Smokes me?" Kate snorted. "Keep dreaming."

"This dream is about to become your nightmare," Miranda shot back.

"Okay, Miranda!" Lizzie said, dragging her best friend away from Kate.

Kate smiled smugly and tossed her hair.

"Don't pay any attention to her," Lizzie told Miranda as she put some real estate between themselves and Kate. "Let's stay focused on the head lifeguard, Tate, and how great it's going to be when he gets here. Think about what lifeguarding means: sun, water, looking cool at the pool . . ."

Just then, a gangly figure in a pair of navy-blue swim trunks and a putty-colored shirt with a puce collar trotted out of the boys' changing room. He was wearing a diving mask pushed back onto the top of his head.

"It gets worse," Miranda said under her breath.

"Hello, Miranda," the dark-haired boy said in an *Am-I-not-suave?* voice as he snapped the mask over his eyes. "Hello, Lizzie."

"Hello, Larry," Lizzie and Miranda replied.

Ooh, this really cuts down on the glamour factor, Lizzie thought as she eyed Larry Tudgeman, King Geek of Hillridge Junior High School. She couldn't believe he was actually wearing his everyday putty shirt at the pool. Does he ever take that thing off? Lizzie wondered. Actually, she thought a moment later, I hope he doesn't.

Lizzie looked at her watch. "Isn't it about time to start?" she asked Miranda.

Miranda shrugged. "Lifeguards are laid-back," she said. "I'm sure Tate is just running a little—"

"Hello, class!" boomed a voice.

Lizzie and Miranda looked up. Oh, no, Lizzie thought as she looked into the craggy face of Coach Kelly—Hillridge Junior High's very own gym teacher. The six-foot-tall Coach Kelly was sporting a flowered green-and-yellow bathing suit with a skirt on it. She pulled her wild brown curls into a tight pony-tail as she grinned at the kids by the side of the pool. "I'm so glad you could all make it to the junior lifeguarding class. For those of you who don't know me, I'm Coach Kelly."

Lizzie's eyes got bigger, and—before she even had a chance to think—she raised her hand in the air hesitantly. "Um, excuse me?"

"Yes, Lizzie?"

"Uh—isn't Tate supposed to be teaching this class?" Lizzie asked. Please tell me he's sick today, she begged silently. Tell me he's running late. Tell me—

"I teach the junior lifeguarding class," Coach Kelly said.

"You teach it," Lizzie repeated.

"I sure do," Coach Kelly said, squaring her massive shoulders. "And the first thing we're all going to do is twenty laps. So, let's hop in the pool and start swimming."

Miranda and Lizzie exchanged a look. Twenty laps? Lizzie thought. What about my leisurely lifeguarding class? What about fun in the sun? What about gazing at Tate all day?

"Um, Coach Kelly?" Kate piped up. "I just spent all morning curling my hair, and I can't really get it wet. I brought a note." She held out a small, white slip of paper.

Coach Kelly cocked an eyebrow, ignoring the note. "Kate, get in the pool," she commanded.

Lizzie couldn't help a small grin as Kate waded gingerly down the pool ladder steps, then dog-paddled furiously, trying to keep her head above water.

Okay, so at least one thing is going right this morning.

"I can't believe we have another hour of this," Miranda griped as she and Lizzie staggered toward the smoothie stand, dripping and exhausted.

"I know," Lizzie agreed. "Coach Kelly's swim class is worse than the obstacle course she made us run at the end of the year. And I didn't think it could get much worse than having to slide through mud under a web of ropes." Lizzie shuddered, remembering the difficult course—there had been tires to run through, ropes to swing on, a wall to scale, and the infamous mud patch.

"Look at it this way," Miranda said, "at least the pool keeps us clean."

"Yeah, but it's twice as hard," Lizzie complained.

"If it weren't for that radio contest—" Miranda grumbled.

"I know, I know," Lizzie agreed. "Just think about the recording studio. Think about performing with Simple Sample. Don't think about the pain."

"I still can't believe she expects us to be able to swim the entire length of the pool without taking a breath," Miranda complained. "I mean, hel-lo—I'm here to learn how to be a lifeguard, not a seal."

"Oh, I know," Lizzie agreed. "And ten minutes of treading water? My thighs are about to fall off."

"If she blows that whistle at me one more time and tells me to watch my form . . ." Miranda growled through clenched teeth as she and Lizzie stepped up to the smoothie stand.

"Hi, guys!" Scott gave them a huge grin.

"*You*," Miranda growled, narrowing her eyes at him.

Scott's smile disappeared. "Uh-oh."

"Why didn't you warn us that this junior lifeguarding class was tougher than basic training?" Miranda demanded.

"We were expecting lessons in whistle twirling and suntan-lotion application," Lizzie griped. "We didn't realize we were entering the Olympic trials."

Scott looked sheepish. "Is it that hard?" he asked.

"That hard?" Lizzie repeated. "I just did twenty-five laps and thirty shallow-water dives. I won't be able to move tomorrow."

"But we'll have to," Miranda said, "because we've got to come back here and do this all over again!"

"Well, at least you're getting into great shape," Scott said.

"Yeah, now if I ever decide to swim to Hawaii, I'll be all set," Lizzie said.

"Would a free smoothie make it up to you?" Scott asked, his hazel eyes twinkling.

Lizzie and Miranda exchanged glances. "You're on," Miranda said. "Raspberry-kiwi."

"Two," Lizzie added.

Scott grinned. "Coming right up."

Miranda flopped onto a stool. "This was a

bad idea," she said. "Now I'll never be able to get up again."

"At least you didn't have Kate trying to sabotage you all morning," Lizzie said, slipping onto the stool beside her friend.

"What do you mean?" Miranda asked.

"You know how she volunteered to put the weights at the bottom of the pool?" Lizzie replied.

"Yeah . . ."

Coach Kelly had asked everyone in the class to retrieve a pair of weights at the bottom of the pool. She was ranking the class on their diving form and speed as they returned to the edge of the pool with the weights.

"Well, I thought it was weird that I could hardly haul my weights out of the pool," Lizzie said, "considering that I have pretty strong arms from wrestling Matt."

"Good point," Miranda said.

"So when I checked my weights, I saw that Kate had set me up with fifteen pounders," Lizzie said. The weights were only supposed to weigh ten pounds each. That meant that Lizzie had been carrying ten more pounds than everyone else!

"No wonder I had to kick like crazy to lift my arms over the edge of the pool," Lizzie said. "I swallowed half the water in the pool trying to catch my breath and ditch those weights."

"Maybe she made a mistake," Miranda suggested.

"Maybe—but I don't think so," said Lizzie. "She was giggling and whispering with Claire and pointing at me. I know she did it on purpose."

Miranda narrowed her eyes. "That evil little—"

"Here you go," Scott said, serving up the

ice-cold smoothies. He held out a bright green cup to Miranda. "The green goes with your cool new bathing suit."

Miranda smiled. "Thanks."

"You're welcome."

Lizzie looked at her best friend. Miranda was definitely not looking her best. Her hair was a damp and disheveled mess, and her bathing suit was wet and sagging in the rear. But she was smiling brilliantly at Scott, and Lizzie could tell he thought she was pretty from the inside out.

"Um, hello?" Kate called from the other end of the counter. "Can we get some service over here?"

"Just a minute," Scott said, then turned back to Miranda and Lizzie. "Listen, I am really sorry that the class is so tough. I didn't know."

"Oh, that's okay," Miranda said. "Actually,

you're right. By the end of it, we'll be junior lifeguards extraordinaire."

"And thanks for the smoothies," Lizzie said as she took a sip of hers.

"No problem," said Scott.

"Hel-lo!" Kate shouted from her end of the bar. "I'm waiting!"

Rolling his eyes, Scott turned to wait on Kate.

Lizzie stared at her friend. "Well?" she asked.

Miranda looked up from sipping her smoothie. "Well what?"

"Well, what about Scott?" Lizzie demanded. "He obviously likes you, and he's totally sweet."

Miranda smiled. "He is pretty sweet," she admitted.

Lizzie knew Scott wasn't a total hottie or anything, not like Tate, with his square jaw, sun-bleached hair, and awesome muscles. Scott had a round face and was a little chubby, not to mention that he always had to wear that goofy orange uniform. But he had beautiful eyes and a great smile—and a super-nice personality. "So . . ." Lizzie said. "Go for it!"

Miranda laughed and shook her head. "Scott's great. But I've already met my dream guy online."

What's the deal with Miranda? it's raining men all of a sudden!

Lizzie sighed, but she knew better than to argue with her best friend. Once the girl had made up her mind, there was no changing it.

Oh, well, Lizzie thought, Scott is really cool. But I guess Internet Boy is cool, too. And it's really up to Miranda.

Too bad. Those free smoothies would have been awesome!

CHAPTER FIVE

"What about, 'Be who you are, you know you're a star'?" Lizzie suggested. She and Miranda were flopped on couches at the Digital Bean, working on the chorus to their latest song. Lizzie had decided that it would make sense to record more than one if they were paying for the studio time, anyway. Besides, the contest said that you could enter up to three songs in the competition. They might as well increase their chances of winning.

"That's good," Miranda said, peering at Lizzie's notebook. " 'Fake people here, fake people there—seems like fake people everywhere,' " she sang, experimenting with the melody.

" 'You don't need to join the crowd,' " Lizzie added, testing the chorus. " 'Just be proud, sing it out loud! Be who you are, you know you're a star. The ones who keep it real go far!' "

"Awesome!" cried Miranda. She high-fived Lizzie. "And I've already got some ideas for cool moves—"

"Hey, guys," Gordo interrupted, flinging himself on the couch beside Lizzie. He looked miserable.

"Uh, Gordo, what's with the baseball cap?" Lizzie asked.

"Yeah," Miranda put in. "I thought you said that professional sports were for people who didn't have the brains to appreciate the national chess championships."

"I've changed my mind," Gordo said, touching his Yankees cap gingerly. "I've decided that athletes are an underappreciated segment of the population."

Lizzie didn't buy it. She knew Gordo was not a hat person any more than he was a sudden sports fan. This could only mean one thing. "Are you trying to hide the haircut my brother gave you?" she asked.

"Absolutely not," Gordo insisted.

"Then let's see it," Miranda said.

"No."

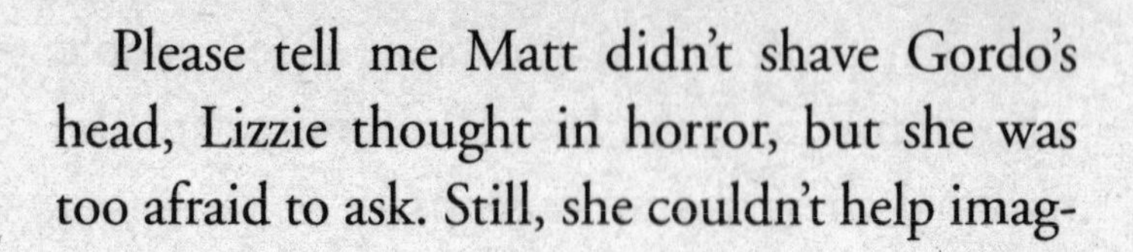

Please tell me Matt didn't shave Gordo's head, Lizzie thought in horror, but she was too afraid to ask. Still, she couldn't help imagining bald patches and awful layers, like the Sneevleys' front yard down the street, which hadn't been mowed in ages, and had been half dug-up by the family's Saint Bernard.

"Gordo, tell me the truth," Miranda said. "Do you or do you not have a Mohawk?"

"It's—" Gordo's head lolled against the back of the couch as he stared at the ceiling in misery. "It's worse than that. . . ."

I can't stand it anymore! Lizzie thought. Unable to stop herself, she snatched Gordo's hat from his head and stared at his hair in shock.

"Whoa . . ." Miranda's eyes bugged out of her head.

"Gordo," Lizzie gasped. "Your hair—"

"It looks *awesome*!" Miranda squealed.

Lizzie nodded in agreement, unable to speak. *Awesome* is actually an understatement, she thought.

Gordo had the coolest haircut she had ever

seen. Like something right out of the $200-a-cut Dominic Dunay Salon. Matt had shaped his curls into attractive layers that brought out the shocking blue of his eyes.

"Your hair looks jamtacular!" Lizzie said.

Gordo groaned. "I know."

"Wait. I don't get it," Miranda said, frowning at Gordo. "You just paid five bucks for the best haircut in the known universe, and you're moping around with a baseball cap on, acting like you just missed winning the lottery by one number."

"Seriously," Lizzie agreed. "If I hadn't taken a solemn oath that Matt would never be allowed to touch my hair again after the honey-on-the-phone-receiver incident, I'd even consider letting him give *me* a haircut. You look great."

"Don't you get it?" Gordo demanded, sitting up straight. "That's the problem!"

Miranda shook her head. "What is?"

"This trendy haircut makes me feel pretentious," Gordo complained. "It's not my style, you know? It doesn't go with the rest of me."

Lizzie sat back, taking in Gordo's whole slump-boy look. She had to admit that he was right. His oversize T-shirt, cargo shorts, tube socks, and high-top sneakers didn't exactly go with his Hollywood hair.

And for the record, i didn't think the word *style* was even in Gordo's vocabulary.

"I guess you do kind of look like you have the wrong head pasted onto your body," Miranda admitted.

"Thanks a lot," Gordo complained.

"But that's easy to fix," Lizzie volunteered. "All it takes is a trip to the mall."

Gordo gave her a dark look. "All it takes is a baseball cap," he said, reaching for the blue-and-white cap in Lizzie's hand.

"Gordo, you can't end your boycott of organized sports just because of one good haircut," Lizzie said.

"Yeah," Miranda agreed. "Besides, your hair is seriously stylin'. You owe it to the world to show it off."

"Well, I do think that professional athletics encourages a herd mentality," Gordo said slowly, half to himself. "And I guess that wearing the hat makes me look like part of the herd. . . ."

"Look, all it takes is one cool pair of jeans and a couple of shirts," Lizzie said. "Then your look will be all at the same level."

"We'll do all the work for you," Miranda volunteered. "We'll be your style consultants."

Gordo looked skeptical. "I don't know. You

aren't going to pick out anything . . . shiny . . . are you?"

"Gordo, we said 'stylish,' not 'ridiculous,'" Lizzie said. "This isn't a reality TV show."

"And no giant belt buckles," Gordo added. "Or glitter."

Miranda gave him a blank look. "You're joking, right?"

"What do you think?" Gordo said, rubbing his hand through his layered brown hair.

I can't believe it, Lizzie thought, watching Gordo muss his hair. That haircut is indestructible! The more Gordo messed with it, the better it looked.

"Maybe it isn't such a bad idea," Gordo said finally. "Okay, let's do it."

The three friends stood up. "So—" Lizzie said as she gathered her notebook and shoved it into her purse. "I'd just like to point out that you're supposed to be broke."

"I *was* broke," Gordo insisted. "But my grandma just sent me a check. My parents told her that I was taking a film class, and she sent me some money for video equipment." Gordo sighed. "But I guess that this is more important right now."

Lizzie laughed. "I can't believe you're actually about to spend money on fashion," she teased. "How does it feel to join us in the shallow end, Gordo?"

"Yeah, who's worried about what other people think now?" Miranda demanded as she pushed open the door to the Digital Bean, and the three friends stepped out into the bright afternoon sun.

"Look, this is a one-time deal," Gordo said, "so that my body matches my head. Besides . . . I have this weird idea that it might make a good subject for my student film."

Lizzie rolled her eyes. Leave it to Gordo to

turn a shopping trip into a film project, she thought.

Still, she couldn't wait to hit the mall.

i just love a makeover project.
Okay, so the project is Gordo.
But still . . .

"I can't believe what she did today!" Lizzie wailed as she flopped onto her bed.

Of course, *she* is Kate.
Or more like she-*beast*.

"Is the girl out to ruin my life?" Lizzie asked. "Or is that just a by-product of her obnoxious personality?"

"Both, I'm pretty sure," said Miranda as

she kicked off her shoes and joined Lizzie on her bed. Miranda had come over to teach Lizzie the dance moves for their latest song . . . but it was obvious that Lizzie needed to vent first.

Lizzie shook her head. "How does she get away with it?"

Coach Kelly had been testing everyone to see who could hold their breath until they reached the far end of the pool. Most people were only making it about two-thirds of the way, except for Larry Tudgeman, who swam the whole length of the pool in one breath on the first try.

Tudgeman probably spent his entire childhood "experimenting" with how long he could hold his breath before he turned blue.

Lizzie had made it three-quarters of the way across the pool. She was pretty sure she'd be able to make it all the way by the end of the week, if she practiced. And, better yet, she was pretty sure that Kate wouldn't make it, even if she spent the whole summer practicing. On her first attempt, Kate had only made it halfway.

But this afternoon, Kate seemed determined. She made a perfect dive into the water, barely causing a ripple. She seemed to shimmer as she swam under the crystal clear surface of the pool.

"Let's see if she makes it past the lifeguard stand," Miranda had whispered to Lizzie, who smiled. The lifeguard stand was the halfway point.

Just as Kate was about to pass the lifeguard stand, Claire let out a little scream, and started batting furiously at an invisible insect.

"A bee!" Claire shouted. "I'm allergic! If a bee stings me, I could die! Get it away! Get it away!"

"Stand still, Claire!" Coach Kelly barked. "It's probably just attracted to your perfume."

"Get it off me!" Claire shook her head frantically and darted away.

Coach Kelly and the other students hurried over to help Claire. But Lizzie remembered that she had a bottle of bug repellent in her bag at the edge of the pool, so she ran in the opposite direction. That was why she saw Kate come up for a quick breath and then keep on swimming. By the time Claire had escaped from her nonexistent bee, Kate was standing in the shallow end of the pool.

"I did it!" Kate shouted in triumph. "I swam the whole way without taking a breath!"

Coach Kelly nodded, looking pretty ragged. She had chased Claire from one end of the pool to the other, trying to calm her down.

"Wait a minute!" Lizzie cried at the coach before she recorded the feat in her notebook. "You're just going to take her word for it?"

Coach Kelly looked confused. "But we just saw her come up."

"But she took a breath while we weren't looking," Lizzie protested. "We were all busy helping Claire, and—"

"She's lying," challenged Kate. "Listen to her. She said it herself. '*We* were all busy helping Claire.' If Lizzie was busy helping Claire, then how did she see me do anything?"

Lizzie sputtered. She turned red. Kate and Claire had set the whole thing up. Lizzie just knew it, but she didn't say it. She was sure Kate would just call her a liar again—and she didn't have any proof.

"What's the big deal?" said Miranda,

coming to Lizzie's aid. "If Kate swam it once with one breath, then she can swim it again."

"I am not swimming the whole length of the pool over again just because Lizzie's a sore loser," Kate insisted, her eyes flashing. "Coach Kelly said we only have to do it once. I did it once—I'm done."

Lizzie wanted to protest again, but she felt like she couldn't. Coach Kelly looked annoyed already, and Lizzie knew she'd probably end up sounding like a sore loser, just like Kate had said.

Now that the class was over for the day, Lizzie felt even worse.

"She can't keep this up forever," Miranda said, crossing her legs on Lizzie's bed. "One of these days, she'll slip up, and then—bam!" She gritted her teeth, her dark eyes flashing.

Lizzie looked dubious. "Bam what?"

"You know, bam. We'll have her," Miranda said. She shrugged as if it were inevitable. Lizzie wasn't so sure.

"I hope you're right," Lizzie said. "I don't know how much more—"

Thump.

Lizzie and Miranda looked at each other.

"Um—what was that?" Lizzie asked.

"It sounds like a football player is trying to break into your room," Miranda said, staring at Lizzie's door, where the noise had come from.

Thump. Thump!

"Matt!" Lizzie shouted. "Get away from my door!"

Thump!

"That's it!" Lizzie hopped off her bed and marched toward the door. "Matt—" she said, yanking it open.

A rubber ball whizzed into her room and

smashed into a pile of CDs on the bureau, knocking them to the ground with a crash. "My Simple Sample CDs!" Lizzie shrieked.

"Sorry!" A redheaded kid scuttled into Lizzie's room to collect his ball.

"Um, hello? Do I know you?" Lizzie asked, frowning at the kid.

"No."

"Then, please exit my room," Lizzie said, pointing to the door.

The kid nodded. "Sorry," he said sheepishly. "I was just practicing handball."

"Do you normally practice handball in people's hallways?" Miranda demanded.

"Well, no," the kid admitted. "But I was afraid that if I went outside, I'd lose my place in line."

"In line?" Lizzie stuck her head out of her doorway, and blinked in surprise.

The hall was packed with kids—the line

stretched all the way down the stairs. Kids were hanging out, napping, playing cards or jacks, flipping through magazines . . . two guys were even tossing around a football.

"What's going on?" Lizzie demanded. "Who are you people?"

A couple of kids looked up at her blankly, but most of them just ignored her. At that moment, Matt's door flew open, and he stuck out his spiky head. "Next!" he shouted.

"That's me," the redheaded kid said, moving toward the door.

"Whoa, whoa, whoa," Lizzie said, grabbing handball boy by the collar. "Next for what?"

"Next for a haircut," the kid explained. "Matt gives the coolest haircuts in town—everyone wants one. And he's only charging eight bucks."

Lizzie looked at Miranda.

"Hey, don't look at me," Miranda said. "I think it's a great deal."

So the rates have gone up already, Lizzie thought as she released the kid, who scurried down the hall toward Matt's door.

There was a loud crash, and Lizzie heard some kid shout, "Sorry!"

"Come on," Lizzie said. There was only one way to put a stop to this—she had to find her mother.

Lizzie and Miranda made their way through the crowd of kids.

"Could you move the magic act somewhere else?" Lizzie griped as she tripped over a girl pulling colored scarves out of a tall black hat. "Thank you. And put that football away before you break something."

Lizzie tramped into the kitchen, where her mom was unloading groceries. "Mom, do you have any idea what's happening upstairs?"

"Matt and Lanny are playing quietly in Matt's room?" Mrs. McGuire guessed cluelessly.

"More like Matt has taken over the house with help from his gang of junior nerds," Lizzie enlightened her.

Mrs. McGuire looked at the ceiling. "One of these days, my guess is going to be correct." Sighing, she trudged to the stairs. "Oh, my—" Squaring her shoulders, Mrs. McGuire tramped up toward Matt's room. "Excuse me," she said to the kids on the stairs. "Could you make a little room? Thanks. Try not to drop crumbs on the carpet, okay? I just vacuumed that. Thank you."

Lizzie followed in her mother's wake, Miranda right behind her. Neither of the girls wanted to miss whatever was going to happen next.

"Matt!" Mrs. McGuire shouted as she reached her son's door. She banged on the door, but there was no answer. Finally, she shoved it open. A blast of classical music rolled over her like a tidal wave. "Turn that off!" she barked.

From his place at the boom box, Lanny pressed the STOP button, and Matt opened his eyes, looking up from his work.

"Mom," Matt griped. "What are you doing? I need the music to *feel* what I'm doing."

"Matt, there is a crowd of kids in the hallway." Mrs. McGuire folded her arms across her chest. "Do you want to tell me what they're doing here?"

"We're getting haircuts!" the redheaded kid in the chair chirped happily. Lizzie had to admit that his hair looked much cooler than it had when he came in.

"I thought you wanted me to make my own money," Matt said to his mother.

"Matt, I think it's great that you're running your own business," Mrs. McGuire told him. "But you and Lanny have to start making appointments. We can't just have a crowd of kids in the hallway."

"Appointments?" Matt wailed. "Mom—you're taking the spontaneity out of my work!" He looked to Lanny for support.

Lanny shrugged.

"Well, Lanny, maybe you're right," Matt said after a moment. "Appointments *would* give me more control. And I could work at a higher level."

Lanny blinked.

"That's true," Matt said thoughtfully. "I could execute my artistic vision more completely, and branch out in new directions. Mom, Lanny has talked me into it. We'll make appointments."

"Good," Mrs. McGuire said. "So maybe you can start now, and send these kids home?"

"Consider it done," Matt said, snapping his fingers.

Lizzie stared at her mother and asked, "So that's it? Matt still gets to run his haircut business out of the house?"

"I don't see why not," Mrs. McGuire said, "as long as it's one kid at a time."

Matt whipped the towel away from the redheaded kid's neck.

"Thanks, Matt!" the kid said enthusiastically as he rubbed his hair. "I love it!"

"My pleasure," Matt said as he held open the door for the kid. "Next!" he shouted.

Lizzie rolled her eyes.

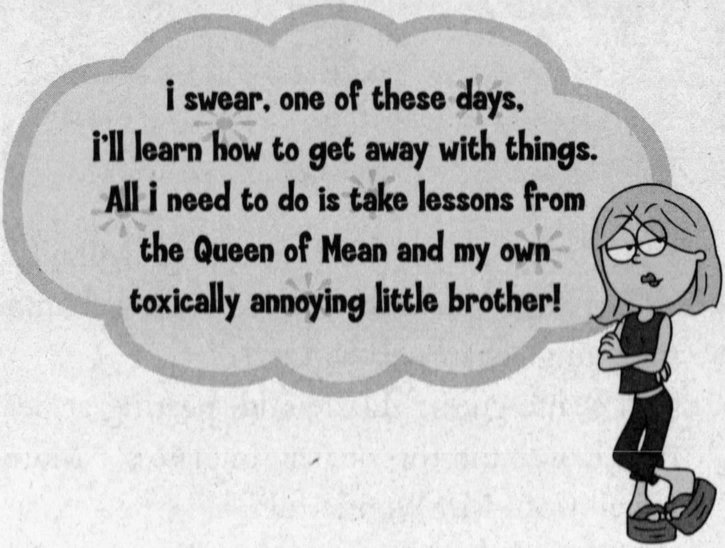

i swear, one of these days,
i'll learn how to get away with things.
All i need to do is take lessons from
the Queen of Mean and my own
toxically annoying little brother!

At the pool the next morning, Miranda wore a huge grin as she flipped her towel onto the lounge chair next to Lizzie's.

"Let me guess," Lizzie said, peering at her friend over the top of her sunglasses. "More e-mail from Mr. Wonderful?"

"I sent him our songs, and he said they were fantastic!" Miranda cried. "He says he thinks we'll definitely win, based on the lyrics alone. Then he sent me a poem he's been working on." Miranda batted her eyes dreamily.

"Wow, you're really crushin' on this guy," Lizzie said.

"He's just so perfect for me," Miranda admitted. "He's funny, and sweet, and smart, and cute—"

"Cute?" Lizzie asked. "Has he sent you a picture, or something?"

"What?" A worry line formed between Miranda's eyebrows. "Well, no . . . I mean, I just think he must be cute. . . . Actually," she admitted, "I have no idea what he looks like." She bit her lip. "Do you think I should be worried?"

"No," Lizzie said.

"I mean, it's not like I'm shallow," Miranda went on.

"Right," Lizzie agreed.

"Then again, what if there's something

really strange about him—like he has two heads?" Miranda asked, her eyes widening in horror.

"Miranda, he doesn't have two heads," Lizzie said reasonably. "If he did, I'm sure he would have mentioned it by now."

"He could have green skin!" Miranda said suddenly. "Or scales. Omigosh, I could be dating Lizard Boy!"

"Miranda, calm down!" Lizzie said.

"How can I calm down when I'm dating a two-headed dinosaur?" Miranda wailed. "I have to find out what he looks like right away!"

For a moment, Lizzie thought Miranda was going to dart off right that minute, but just then, Coach Kelly thundered out of the pool house with her clipboard. "All right, every-one!" she boomed. "Listen up! This week, we're going to focus on CPR. We're going to be practicing lifesaving and resuscitation techniques, so I want everyone to buddy up. When I call your name, tell me who your buddy is."

That's easy, Lizzie thought, turning toward Miranda and smiling.

"I took a lifesaving course last year, when I was working as a babysitter," Miranda whispered.

"Piece of cake," Lizzie agreed. She had learned the basics of lifesaving in health class. Not only that, Lizzie had actually saved a man from choking at a local movie theater by using the Heimlich maneuver. It had been on the news and everything. Of course, that had gotten her into major trouble with her parents, since she had been trying to sneak into the R-rated movie *Vesuvius* at the time, but it was still worth it.

"Claire?" the coach shouted.

"Jen Miller," Claire said, naming a tall, athletic girl with short brown hair.

Jen? Lizzie thought, frowning. Why didn't Claire partner with Kate? Strange things are afoot at the pool, Lizzie thought, narrowing her eyes at Kate.

"Kate?" Coach Kelly called.

"Miranda Sanchez!" Kate shouted.

What! Lizzie and Miranda gaped at each other. This has got to be another one of Kate's evil tricks.

"Wait a minute," Lizzie piped up. "I want to partner with Miranda."

"Yeah," Miranda agreed. "Lizzie and I are buddies."

Coach Kelly looked annoyed. "That's sweet, you two. But you won't always get to choose whose life you save. Miranda, you're with Kate." She made a note on her clipboard. "And now Lizzie McGuire needs a partner, people," the coach announced. "Any takers?"

Lizzie looked hopefully at Veronica Peters, a shy girl with curly hair. Okay, so I've never spoken to you in my life, Lizzie thought, but you've got to come through for me now, or else I could end up with—

"I'll be Lizzie's partner," said a voice.

"Larry Tudgeman," Coach Kelly said, scribbling something on her clipboard. "Thanks for stepping up."

Larry smiled flirtatiously at Lizzie.

Oh, no, Lizzie thought, her stomach sinking. Please tell me I'm not going to have to perform mouth-to-mouth on Larry.

Just then, as though he had read her mind, Larry pulled a small canister out of the pocket of his swim trunks and squirted himself twice in the mouth.

Breath spray, Lizzie thought in horror.

Call me crazy, but since when do lessons in *life*saving have to include a fate worse than *death*?

Lizzie narrowed her eyes at Kate, who smiled smugly then jerked her thumb at Larry and pursed her lips in a mocking kissy face.

Oooooh! You just wait, Kate Sanders. This isn't over yet.

"Well, that was awful," Miranda said as she and Lizzie flopped onto parallel lounge chairs.

Lizzie stared into the crystal water. "I don't want to talk about it."

"Kate refused to even try the mouth-to-mouth," Miranda griped, ignoring Lizzie. She said she didn't want to smudge her lip gloss!"

"This is *not* 'not talking about it,'" Lizzie pointed out.

"Now I have a minus for the day," said Miranda, then she folded her arms across her chest and smiled. "But at least Kate does, too."

"Look, I don't think you understand," Lizzie said, sitting up straight to look her friend full in the face. "My lips and Tudgeman's touched the same lifesaving dummy. That's practically contact!" Lizzie shuddered. Okay, so it wasn't as bad as she had feared it would be—they'd only had to share a dummy, not practice on each other. Still. Larry had kept correcting Lizzie's CPR form—and that meant putting his hands over hers as she pumped the dummy's chest—and breathing his minty breath as he cheered her on. "So can we please not talk about it? I don't want to relive the horror." The minty, minty horror, Lizzie thought. *Blech.*

"Look on the bright side," Miranda said. "You got a plus for the day. Now you're even with Kate." She dug around in her tote bag and pulled out a music magazine. Jyll Hyde was on the cover—looking jamtacular, of course.

"Yeah, but we're both behind Tudgeman," Lizzie pointed out. "And only one person can get that assistant lifeguard position."

Miranda snorted. "We need that money for our music careers," she pointed out as she flipped idly through her magazine. "What would Larry do with the money from the job, anyway?" she asked.

"He told me he wants to buy a life-size rubber model of Jabba the Hut that he found on eBay," Lizzie said, settling back on her chair.

Miranda looked blank. "I can't believe that there's actually someone in this world who would pay money for that."

The next day, Lizzie and Miranda were lounging by the pool after a long class. "Hey, guys," Gordo said as he walked up to them—or, at least it *sounded* like Gordo, thought Lizzie. But he sure didn't look like the Gordo she knew. He wore dark sunglasses, a black short-sleeved button-down shirt, baggy khaki swim trunks, and a pair of black "mandals"—open-toed men's sandals—that Lizzie had picked out for him at the mall despite Gordo's protests that he lived in Hillridge, not a Kenneth Cole ad.

All of that, combined with the Matt haircut, equaled one mighty fine, Hollywood-cool Gordo. Lizzie couldn't help grinning at him as he sat down on the edge of her lounge chair.

"Oh, look, Captain Fashion has come to pay us a visit," Miranda teased.

"Yeah, Gordo. It's like every day is Halloween," Lizzie added. "In a good way."

Gordo looked at her over the top of his sunglasses. "I don't really know how I could take that in a good way," he said.

"Hey, Gordo!" A blond girl in a leopard-print bikini waved at Gordo as she walked past.

"Oh, hey." Gordo leaned back on his elbows and peered up at the girl through his dark glasses.

The image of cool, Lizzie thought, watching him.

"What have you been up to this summer?" the girl asked. "I haven't seen you around."

"Oh, you know, this and that. Taking a film class," Gordo said, gesturing to his video camera.

"Wow." The girl's eyes went wide with admiration. "That is so cool. Well, look, I gotta run. Maybe I'll give you a call, and we could hang out."

"Sounds great," Gordo said, giving the girl a casual wave as she walked off.

"Who was that?" Lizzie asked once the girl was out of earshot.

"No idea," Gordo said.

"Gordo, my man!" A tall, dark, and handsome dude, whom Lizzie didn't know, walked up to Gordo and laid a high five on him.

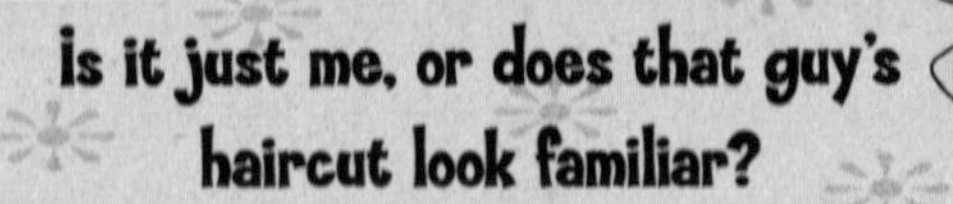

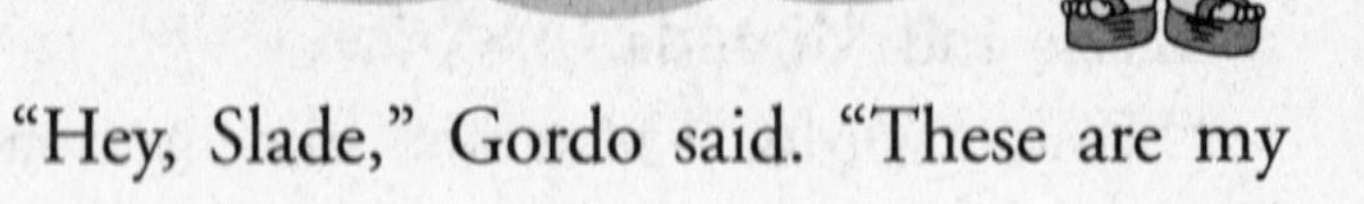

"Hey, Slade," Gordo said. "These are my

friends, Lizzie and Miranda. Slade is in my film class," Gordo explained, catching the introduction on film.

"Ladies," Slade said smoothly, giving Lizzie and Miranda a megawatt smile. "Gordo, man, I'm having a party this weekend. It would be awesome if you could make it. My house, live band, and plenty to eat—my mom owns a restaurant."

"What restaurant?" Miranda asked.

"Annabelle's," Slade said.

Lizzie's eyes went wide. *Annabelle's?* she thought. *They have the best barbecue in town! And live music, too—I'm there!*

"Sounds good," Gordo said. "I'll try to stop by."

"Dude, that would be way awesome!" Slade said. "Bring your buds," he added, gesturing to Lizzie and Miranda.

"Wow, Gordo," Miranda said as Slade

headed toward the smoothie stand. "You sure are making some cool friends."

"Was that guy wearing your hair?" Lizzie asked.

"I'm telling you, it's my new look." Gordo's eyes were shining. "Everyone wants to hang out with me. So far, three of the guys in my film class have gone to Matt for haircuts. It's way awesome!"

"Way awesome?" Lizzie repeated.

Gordo is flipping over good hair? Could it be he's been spending a little too much time in the sun?

"I thought it bugged you when other people copied your look," Miranda pointed out.

Lizzie nodded. A while back, Gordo had started wearing clothing from the fifties and listening to music from that era—especially songs recorded by a group of Vegas entertainers known as the Rat Pack. He was the only one doing it at first, but then everyone started doing it, too. And that made Gordo angry. He hated being part of a crowd, so he dropped his new Rat Pack hobby, saying he didn't want to follow a trend—even though he'd been the one to start it.

"But this is just fashion," Gordo argued. "It's not like it's my original look, or anything. It's just stuff I bought at the mall."

"And so it doesn't bother you that other people are starting to look like you?" Lizzie asked.

Gordo shrugged. "It's interesting. One cool haircut, and everyone is starting to notice me and dress like me. Oh, great," he said, grabbing Miranda's music magazine. "An article on what rock stars are wearing. I need that."

"Uh, hel-lo?" Lizzie said, giving Gordo a skeptical look. "Gordo, are you *in* there? Because this guy who has taken over your body is really into fashion, and it's kind of creeping me out."

"You're not getting this," Gordo said. "This is the whole idea—people are treating me differently because of how I look. When I wore whatever I wanted, and had bad hair, the 'cool' kids didn't give me the time of day. But now that I've got what looks like a two-hundred-dollar cut and I'm wearing 'mandals,' they all want to hang out."

"No, *you're* not getting it, Gordo," Miranda said, grabbing back her magazine. "What we think is weird is the fact that you, Gordo, are suddenly so *into* being popular. Why?"

"Because I'm capturing the magic on film!" Gordo said, holding up his video camera. "It's perfect—I'm an undercover nerd! Oh, hey," he said to himself. "That's a good title for my documentary."

"Gordo!" A girl with long brown hair was waving at him from the other side of the pool.

"Hey!" Gordo stood up and held his video camera's viewfinder to his eyes. "Gotta get to work," he whispered to Miranda and Lizzie before straightening up and walking off to join the girl.

"Is Gordo an evil genius?" Lizzie asked as she watched him sit down with the long-haired girl. He said something and she laughed.

"Pretty much," Miranda replied, then looked down at her magazine.

"Don't look now," Lizzie said, catching sight of a familiar orange cap near the diving board.

"At what?" Miranda asked, her head snapping to attention.

Lizzie closed her eyes and shook her head. "That's really subtle, Miranda."

"You know me—queen of keeping it on the down low," Miranda said, craning her neck. "What am I looking at?"

"Scott is delivering smoothies to those two guys near the diving board," Lizzie said. "But he's looking this way. At *you*."

Miranda smiled and waved at Scott, who looked kind of embarrassed but waved back, anyway. "He's a sweetie," Miranda said.

"Why don't you go over and say hi?" Lizzie suggested.

"Eh," Miranda said, shrugging. "I'm really into Blaine right now."

Lizzie's eyebrows drew together in confusion. "Blaine?"

"My online hottie," Miranda explained. She rummaged around in her tote bag and came up with a sheet of paper. "After we talked yesterday, I decided I'd better find out what he looked like. So I asked him to zap me a picture. Check him out." Miranda handed the printout to Lizzie.

"Whoa," Lizzie said. This guy was a hunk and a half—the photo he had sent was of him at the beach. He was tan and muscular, and his piercing green eyes gazed steadily at the camera, over a cocky smile. Blaine was standing next to a surfboard, and seemed pretty tall, and maybe a little older. "I didn't know your guy was into surfing."

"Yeah, he told me all about it after he sent the photo," Miranda said. "I guess he's kind of into sports."

Lizzie nodded. That would make sense, given how strong he looks, she thought. "He looks kind of familiar," Lizzie said after a moment.

"I thought so, too," Miranda agreed.

"There's something about him. . . . Anyway, I can't believe I've finally found Mr. Perfect!"

Virtually found him, Lizzie thought, looking at the picture. She thought it was funny that Miranda could be so excited about a guy she'd never actually met in person. Still, Lizzie had to admit that he did seem pretty perfect—he was funny, he volunteered with kids, and he was Grade-A gorgeous.

She looked up at Scott, who was heading back to the snack counter to finish his shift. Poor guy, Lizzie thought as she watched him. He can't really compete with all that.

Although he does make a really mean smoothie.

"Hey, Gordo," Lucy said when he walked into class the next day. She had saved him a seat, as usual. "I didn't know you were a fan of Japanese baseball." Lucy eyed his red shirt.

Gordo looked down at his shirt, which had HIROSHIMA CARP written across the front. "Is that what this is?" he asked. "My friend picked this out for me."

Lucy laughed. "You're not really into shopping, are you?"

"Not really," Gordo admitted, giving her a lopsided grin. "Unless it's for CDs or video equipment."

"How's the documentary coming?" Lucy asked. "I'm ready for my close-up."

Gordo shifted in his seat uncomfortably. He didn't really want anyone in his film class to know what he was doing. After all, this was where he was getting some of his best material. And he didn't really know Lucy that well yet. Even though he was pretty sure she would keep his secret, he didn't want anything to slip out. "Well . . . actually," Gordo hedged, "it's taken on kind of a new twist. . . ."

"Hey, Gordo." A guy with Gordo hair walked past.

"Hey," Gordo said.

"Something very interesting has happened to the hairstyles in this class," Lucy observed, scanning the rows of kids in front of them.

Two more people—a guy and a girl—had gotten Matt haircuts. "I feel like I'm in some kind of freaky clone movie."

Gordo had to laugh. "Well, your hairstyle is stolen from Cleopatra," he pointed out.

"True," Lucy admitted. "Remind me to hack it off if she ever shows up in this class." She grinned. Today, Lucy was wearing a white sundress with giant red tomatoes printed on it. Gordo doubted anyone else in the class would copy her outfit.

"Hey, Gordo!" two girls chorused from the front row. "Love your shirt!" the redhead said. She was the one whose hair looked like Gordo's.

"It's a Japanese baseball shirt," Gordo told them.

Lucy frowned at him.

"I *love* Japanese baseball," the blond girl said brightly.

"Oh, really?" Lucy asked. "What's your favorite team?"

The blond girl blinked blankly. She ignored Lucy. "See you after class, Gordo," the girl said, and she and her redheaded friend turned back around.

"Hmm," Lucy said dryly, "something tells me that they aren't really huge fans."

She said it jokingly, but Gordo could see Lucy looked kind of hurt. Given how those girls had just blown her off, it was understandable.

Lucy sighed. "Listen," she said after a moment, "do you want to hit the Noir Film Festival at the Sharpstown Theater later? *Wait Until Dark* is playing—one day only."

"Oh, man, *Wait Until Dark* is one of my favorites," Gordo said.

"It's playing at four. We can just go over after class," Lucy suggested.

Gordo winced. "Actually, I have plans . . ."

Lucy lifted her eyebrows, but all she said was, "Oh."

"We're going to see *Nightflame*," Gordo explained, his face flushing slightly with embarrassment.

"We?"

Gordo gestured to the two girls in the front row. They had asked him the day before. "You can come along, if you want," Gordo said quickly, then instantly regretted it. For one thing, he was pretty sure that Lucy would find Cindy (the redhead) and Heather (the blond) pretty annoying. The truth was, *Gordo* found them kind of annoying—especially since they'd never even said hello to him until he changed his hair and his clothes. But even worse, *Nightflame* was a comic-book action hero, and the movie was a big-budget Hollywood-style summer flick, complete with an explosion every thirty seconds. It wasn't exactly Lucy's kind of movie.

"I think I'll pass," Lucy said, her eyes clouding over.

"Maybe we could hit the film festival another day," Gordo suggested.

"Yeah, maybe," Lucy said, although she didn't sound excited about it.

Gordo was about to tell her that he would check the schedule and see what else was playing, but just then, Hathaway walked in. "All right, class," he said, stepping to the front of the room in one of his usual undertaker-inspired outfits. "Today, we're going to discuss writing dialogue. . . ."

Gordo sat back in his chair, thinking about how much he would rather see *Wait Until Dark* with Lucy than *Nightflame* with Cindy and Heather. And he felt kind of bad—because he could tell that Lucy was disappointed.

But, Gordo thought, sometimes a filmmaker had to suffer. And that was what he was willing to do. All in the name of art.

Lizzie took a deep breath as Coach Kelly scowled at the clipboard in her hand. Today was the day—the final day of junior lifeguarding class—and Coach Kelly was going to name the top student. And then we'll know whether Miranda and I are headed for stardom . . . or whether we need to start shopping for a karaoke-machine rental.

"I'm totally cool with whatever she says," Lizzie told Miranda.

"Well, I have some very interesting news," Coach Kelly announced.

And if it isn't me, for heaven's sake, don't let it be Kate!

Miranda gripped Lizzie's hand tightly. The two girls had tried over and over to calculate who was in the lead—but their answers kept coming up differently. Once, they figured out that it had to be Lizzie. The next time, they thought it was Larry. And then they thought it might be Kate. . . .

The suspense is killing me!

"It seems we have a three-way tie for top student," Coach Kelly announced. "Lizzie McGuire, Larry Tudgeman, and Kate Sanders."

Miranda gripped Lizzie's hand harder. Then she piped up. "So do they all get the job?"

Coach Kelly shook her head. "There can only be one. So—" She gestured toward the pool, which was split in half by the length of a water polo net. "I've come up with one more test. Whoever wins this, wins the whole thing."

"But—but that's not fair," Larry griped. "If the differential between our scores is really so low, statistically speaking—"

"Save it for your math class, Tudgeman," the coach told him, holding up a hand. "This is the way it's going to work. I've clipped three hooks onto the net. Each of you will swim to the net, grab one of the hooks, swim under the net and all the way to the other end of the pool. Then you must toss out the hook, take only one breath, and swim all the way back to the other end. I'll be timing you. Whoever has the fastest time wins."

Oh, great, Lizzie thought. She hated that thing where you had to swim the length of the pool in only one breath. But still, after two weeks of practice, she knew she could do it. She also knew that Kate probably couldn't. She looked over at Miranda who nodded encouragingly.

I can do it, Lizzie told herself. After all, I've been working hard in this class, I really like to help people—

Suddenly, there was a shriek from the edge of the pool. "My earring!" Claire cried. "It fell out—we have to find it!"

"Claire, can't this wait?" Coach Kelly demanded.

"I inherited those earrings from my grandmother," Claire said.

Lizzie had to bite back a groan as she and Miranda exchanged glances. Lizzie didn't believe Claire's story for a second. She didn't know what Claire was up to, but Lizzie was pretty sure it must involve helping Kate. Or sabotaging her competitors. Or both.

The coach sighed. "All right, everybody," she said in a tired voice, "let's find the earring."

Lizzie rolled her eyes.

"Keep an eye on Claire," Miranda commanded in a whisper. "I'll watch Kate." She narrowed her eyes. "Just remember—bam."

Lizzie nodded. *Bam,* we'll have her, she thought. *Maybe.*

"I think it might have dropped over by these bushes," Claire said, pointing to the shrubs near the fence.

Dutifully, all of the junior lifeguards trekked over to look for the earring. Lizzie tried to search near Claire. . . . She noticed that Kate was still by the edge of the pool. Miranda was right next to her.

But Lizzie wasn't the only one who had noticed.

"Miranda! Kate!" Coach Kelly barked. "Less standing around—more searching."

Miranda's mouth dropped open. "But I—"

"I'm trying to see if the earring fell into the water," Kate volunteered.

"Fine—you look in the water, Kate. Miranda, you come and join us by the fence," the coach ordered.

Miranda flashed Lizzie a regretful look, but trudged over to the fence.

Lizzie was finding it hard to watch Claire from where she was searching by the fence. Miranda looked over and shook her head. With her back to the pool, she couldn't keep an eye on Kate at all!

"Oh! I found it!" Claire said after a few minutes. "Oh, thanks, everyone!"

There were murmurs of relief as the class headed back to the pool.

"Okay, great—that's over," Coach Kelly said. "Now, let's get on with the last test. Who wants to go first?"

"I think we should go in alphabetical order," Kate volunteered.

"Fine," Coach Kelly nodded. "McGuire, that's you."

"You can do it, Lizzie," Miranda whispered as Lizzie stepped to the lip of the pool and took a deep breath. "You're the best—you deserve it."

Just concentrate, Lizzie told herself. Focus. She crouched to dive in. She stared into the water, which flashed brilliantly in the sun. Her own face looked back at her from the surface. This is it, Lizzie told herself.

"Hold on a minute, there, McGuire," Coach Kelly said. "Let me show you what I want you to do. It's a little complicated."

"What?" Kate said. "Wait—"

But Coach Kelly wasn't listening. She had already dived in, and was taking huge freestyle strokes toward the water polo net. Once she was directly beneath it, she looked up at the hooks hanging from the net. With a quick motion, she grabbed the net in one hand and reached up with the other . . . and a moment later, one side of the net had fallen on her head.

"Omigosh!" Larry cried as everyone at the side of the pool let out a cry of surprise.

"Whoa!" the coach cried as she splashed around, trapped like a fish. "Help!" As she struggled, the net wrapped itself more tightly around her.

"She's panicking!" Larry shouted. "What do we do—she's panicking!"

"Dive in and save her!" Miranda shouted.

"But if she's panicking, she could drag me down, too!" Larry cried, wide-eyed.

"Could someone help me out of here?" Coach Kelly shouted, still struggling with the net.

"Call 911!" Larry shouted.

"I'm on it!" Kate hollered, whipping out her cell phone.

Ignoring the chaos around her, Lizzie grabbed a long-handled hook from the rack on the side of the lifeguard stand. Planting her feet firmly at the edge of the pool, Lizzie held out the hook to Coach Kelly, who grabbed on.

Using her now-strong arm muscles, Lizzie hauled the coach to the side of the pool. *Wow—all of that lap swimming really paid off!* Lizzie thought as Miranda helped her untangle the coach from the net. After a few minutes, they got her untied, and Lizzie pulled the net up over the side of the pool.

"That was quick thinking, McGuire," Coach Kelly said as she hauled herself up the pool ladder. "Good lifeguarding instincts." She stood there, huge and dripping, beaming at Lizzie. She shook her head. "I just don't understand how that could have happened. I tied those knots myself. I know they were secure."

"Er—Coach Kelly?" Larry said sheepishly. "I don't think I want to be the assistant lifeguard. You can take my name off the list."

"I think that's wise, Mr. Tudgeman," Coach Kelly replied.

Sirens wailed as a fire truck pulled up to the front of the pool.

"Um . . . I'll go tell them that we're good here," Kate volunteered.

"Good idea," Miranda told her. "And while you're at it, why don't you keep walking?"

Kate's eyes widened.

"That's right, Kate," Miranda snapped. "Coach?" she said. "The only person who could have loosened the net is the one person who was standing by the pool while we all searched for Claire's earring."

The coach turned to Kate, glowering. "Is that true, Kate?"

"Well, I—" Kate glared at Miranda. "Well, no! Of course not!" She tried to laugh, but it came out sounding tinny.

"She's been cheating all summer," Miranda went on. "Switching Lizzie's weights for heavier ones, smearing suntan lotion on the balls so that they're harder for everyone to grab . . . and now this. That's why she always volunteers for everything. She can't even swim the length of the whole pool without taking a breath."

"That is such a lie," Kate insisted nervously.

Coach Kelly narrowed her eyes.

"Well, now is your chance to prove it," Lizzie said brightly. "Why don't you swim the whole pool in one breath?"

Kate clenched her fists and glared at Lizzie. But there was nothing she could say. There was no way she could swim the entire pool in one breath—and everyone knew it. All she could do was stomp away.

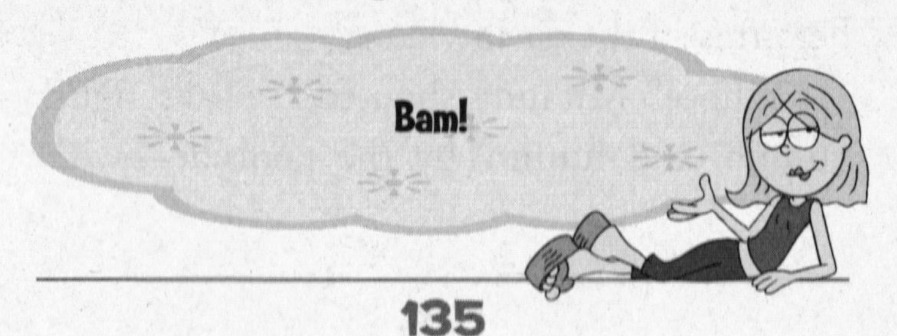

"I should have figured it out a long time ago," Coach Kelly said, shaking her head as she watched Kate storm away. Claire hurried after her like a pathetic little dingy in the *Titanic*'s wake. "I had always suspected that she cheated on that obstacle course at the end of the year, too," the coach confessed. "Too bad I can't change her grade in that class, as well."

Wow, Lizzie thought, looking up at Coach Kelly, *and I always thought that teachers were supposed to be clueless.*

"Well, Lizzie," Coach Kelly said, shoving her wet, curly hair away from her craggy face. "I guess that means you're the new assistant lifeguard. The job is yours, if you want it."

"Really?" Lizzie grinned as Miranda threw her arms in the air in victory.

"Whoo!" Miranda shouted. "That's right! Sunnin' and funnin' by the poolside—with money to burn! And I'll be right by your side the whole time," she promised.

"It'll be like we're both working here!"

"We're gonna be stars!" Lizzie cried.

She and Miranda exchanged a high five.

That recording contract is going to be ours, thought Lizzie. Now all she had to do was earn the money for the demo. And her new job would see to that!

"What about that one?" Miranda asked, pointing to the computer screen. Lizzie had Googled the words "recording studio," and had come up with fifteen matches in three nearby cities.

Lizzie clicked on the name of the studio Miranda was pointing to and started to surf its site. "Six hundred dollars?" she said miserably, adding up the costs for renting the space and using studio musicians for three hours.

"Next!" Miranda declared and took a sip of her soda.

Lizzie went back to the Google list, wiping her damp bangs out of her eyes as she scanned the matches. She and Miranda had spent all morning running through their songs. The good news: their harmonies were hot and their moves were tight. They were definitely ready to record. The bad news: it looked like renting studio space was going to be even more expensive than they thought, especially after they added in the cost of the musicians.

I don't think I did this much math during the entire school year, Lizzie thought as she glanced at the calculations on the notepad beside her computer mouse. She and Miranda had figured out that Lizzie would earn a little more than six hundred dollars after working at the pool for a month. Plus, they wanted to get some cool outfits and have their photo taken for the cover of their demo CD. And it was all adding up to a major expense.

i'll never have enough money to go to another movie in my life.

"Well, this one is a little less expensive," Lizzie said as she scanned the latest site.

"Still five hundred dollars," Miranda pointed out. "Next."

Lizzie tucked her hair behind her ear and shoved her chair away from the desk. "I'm dying of thirst. Take the wheel for a minute?"

"No problemo, chica," Miranda said as she slipped into the desk chair. "Let's try something new." She typed the word *cheap* after *recording studio* in the Google search, and a bunch of new sites popped up.

"You're a genius," Lizzie told her friend.

Miranda shrugged. "Who knows what cheap means to these people," she pointed out. "Get me another soda?" She held up her empty can.

"Be right back," Lizzie said. Hurrying into the kitchen, she grabbed a couple of ginger ales. Just as she turned around, she saw Matt and Lanny walking toward the back door. Matt was carrying a large boom box, and Lanny had a pair of garden shears. "What are you two little freakazoids doing?" Lizzie asked them.

"Um, nothing." Matt said.

Lanny nodded.

Lizzie narrowed her eyes. "Is this 'nothing-nothing' or 'Mom-and-Dad-are-out-of-the-house-and-now-Matt-does-something-strange-and-Lizzie-gets-blamed-for-it-nothing'?"

Matt and Lanny stared at each other. Matt shrugged. "We're going to do some yard work."

"Right," Lizzie said, eyeing the small pair of hand shears in Lanny's hand. "Yard work. Okay. Look—Mom and Dad just went to the store. They'll be back in fifteen minutes, so if you do anything that's going to cause floods, fires, or require an expensive legal defense team, they're going to find out about it. Got it?"

Matt and Lanny looked at each other again. Matt nodded. "Got it."

"Good," Lizzie said. She watched as Matt and Lanny walked out onto the back deck. *Well, whatever it is they're doing,* Lizzie thought, *it can't be as bad as the time they decided to flood the backyard so they could charge the kids in the neighborhood for gondola rides.*

Miranda was staring at the computer screen as Lizzie walked into the living room. "Omigosh!" Miranda said. Wide-eyed, she turned to Lizzie. "Omigosh!" she repeated.

"What is it?" Lizzie asked, hurrying over to the computer. "Did you find a studio space?"

"What?" Miranda asked. "Oh, no—it's not that. I decided to take a break and check my e-mail. And I got a message from Blaine. He wants to meet me. In person!"

"He does?" Lizzie said. She put the sodas on the table, leaned over Miranda's chair, and began to read the screen aloud.

"Hey, Miranda! What's up? I've been thinking

we should hang out sometime. What are you doing on Friday?"

"See what I mean about the Omigosh!" squealed Miranda. "What am I going to wear? What are we going to do? What should I say?"

"I don't know," Lizzie said slowly. She could see her friend was freaking—in a good way. But Lizzie was worried.

"What's wrong?" Miranda asked. "You look weird."

"It's just that . . ." Lizzie bit her lip. "I mean, you don't really know the guy. You should probably meet him in a public place."

"Duh! Of course!" Miranda said, rolling her eyes. "Please, I'm not a *total* bubblehead. I'm not going to run off and meet some guy from the Internet in a dark alley—even if he is from a super-screened middle-school chat room."

"Okay, so—what about the pool?" Lizzie

suggested. "That way, I could be there, too—you know, in the background. And if he seems seriously creepy or anything, I'll just come over and make some excuse so you can leave."

"Perfect!" Miranda said. Then she clicked REPLY, typed a response, and sent the e-mail on its way. "Omigosh, now I have total outfit stress. You *have* to come over and help me pick something out."

Lizzie smiled. "Easy. This is going to be jamtacular! And I'm so glad that I get to check him out, too."

"Hands off, he's mine," Miranda teased.

"Do you want to run through the song a couple more times before we head over to dig through your closet?" Lizzie suggested.

"Sounds great." Miranda hauled herself out of the chair. "I'm too excited to sit still, anyway."

The girls headed to the middle of the living

room and struck their opening poses. But just as they were about to dive into the lyrics, classical music blasted through the open window.

"Matt," Lizzie growled, shutting the window, but it was no use. She could still hear the music and the *snip-snip* of hedge clippers.

"There's no way I can dance to that," Miranda said.

Letting out an "Arrrgh!" Lizzie stormed through the kitchen and out to the rear deck. Miranda was right behind her.

"Matt," Lizzie screeched as she tore through the sliding door, "you'd better shut that off or you're—" Stopping, Lizzie stared at her brother in horror.

"Whoa," Miranda said.

Matt had snipped away at the hedges along the rear fence, which were now in the shape of rolling waves.

Lanny was sitting cross-legged at the end of the yard, the boom box still blasting away in his lap.

"What are you doing?" Lizzie cried as her brother continued to hack away—eyes closed—at the shrubbery. "Shut that off," she commanded, pointing at Lanny.

Lanny obeyed.

"Hey," Matt said, turning to his sister. "I need that music for my inspiration."

"Inspiration?" Lizzie demanded. "Do you have any idea how dead you are? Mom planted those bushes herself—she's going to freak when she sees this."

"I can't help the fact that I'm an artist," Matt insisted. "I need to express myself."

"What's going on out here?" asked a voice behind Lizzie. "Oh my—"

"Mom," Lizzie said as she turned to see her parents staring slack-jawed at the bushes. "I just want you to know that Miranda and I are in no way involved in this."

"Son, what are you doing?" asked Mr. McGuire.

"Expressing myself through the shears," Matt replied, snapping the tool open and closed for emphasis. *Snick, snick!*

Lizzie's mother just shook her head, completely speechless.

"I told him not to do it," Lizzie said.

"It's beautiful," Mrs. McGuire said in a hushed voice.

For a moment, everyone was silent. Then Lizzie blurted out, "You've got to be kidding?!"

"I love it," Mrs. McGuire said, crossing over to the bushes. "It looks like a painting of rolling hills, or waves. Matt," she said, sweetly cupping her son's chin in her hand, "did you do this all by yourself?"

"Lanny helped with the music," said Matt, sheepishly blinking big, innocent eyes.

"It really looks good, son," Mr. McGuire put in.

Lizzie tried not to gag. "Mom, Dad, you can't be serious!" she cried.

Matt hacks up the bushes, and my parents think it's *beautiful*. The world has gone insane!

Lizzie was totally outraged. Her mother and father, however, were obviously not. "You're not even going to punish him?" she wailed.

"Punish him for what?" asked Mr. McGuire. "I've been meaning to trim those hedges for weeks."

"You know, you could pitch in around the house a little, too," Mrs. McGuire told Lizzie.

"I'm not done yet," Matt said. "So can I please have my music? I can't cut without it."

"By all means," said Mrs. McGuire.

Lanny pumped up the volume on the Beethoven.

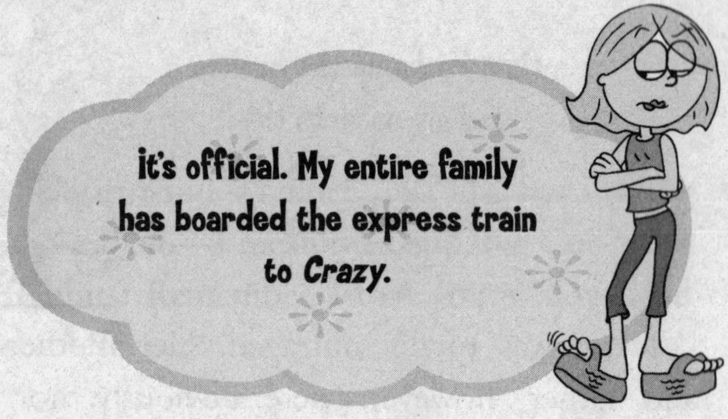

it's official. My entire family has boarded the express train to *Crazy*.

Lizzie sighed. "Come on, Miranda," she said. "Let's go practice our songs at your house. At least your parents aren't nuts."

Miranda raised an eyebrow. "Says you."

* * *

"Oh, no." Gordo let out a groan as he walked up to the mile-long movie line. He had agreed to meet some of the guys from film class here, but it looked like they were already too late. That was a serious bummer, because Gordo was the one who had suggested the movie—the original *D.O.A.*, which was playing at the Noir Festival—and now it looked like it might be sold out. The others had wanted to check out *Thunder Afternoon* at the multiplex. Gordo wondered if he should have just said yes, after all. Then again, *Nightflame* had been so lame, and *Thunder Afternoon* was supposed to be even worse. Gordo wasn't sure he could deal with another mindless action film just a few days after the first one.

Sighing, Gordo looked around. Slade, Heather, and Cindy weren't there yet, so he whipped out his video camera and started filming the craziness on the line. Some of the people were actually dressed as characters from the movie, Gordo noticed, smiling. That was what he loved about film festivals—people really got into them.

"Gordo!"

Gordo looked up to see Lucy waving at him. She was standing with a small knot of people toward the front of the line. "Hey, Gordo!" Lucy bounced over to join him.

"Hey," Gordo said with a smile, "I should have known I'd see you here."

"My friends and I have been waiting in line for two hours," Lucy admitted. "I think they're ready to kill me, but I keep telling them that the movie is excellent, so . . ." She shrugged. "Hopefully, some soda and popcorn will calm them down. I think the ushers are about to start letting people in. Are you here by yourself?"

"I'm supposed to be meeting some people

here," Gordo admitted, scanning the line again. Still no sign of Slade. Gordo wondered whether he was being stood up.

"If they don't show, why don't you join us?" Lucy volunteered, pointing toward her friends.

"Thanks," Gordo said warmly. "That would be really great."

"We'll save you a seat," Lucy told him. Flashing him a smile, she hurried off to rejoin her friends.

"Gordo!" A heavy hand slapped him on the back, and Gordo turned to see Slade standing behind him. Heather and Cindy were with him, and so was another guy from their class—Jim Lu. They all had Gordo hair. The weird thing about Matt's Gordo-style haircut was that it looked equally good on everyone—girls and guys.

"Hey, guys," Gordo said, still peering

through the viewfinder of his video camera.

"Let's head," Slade said to Gordo.

"Oh, they aren't letting anyone in yet," Gordo told him. "Actually, I'm not even sure we'll get in—"

"Don't sweat it," Slade said, "we've got the hookup."

"Slade knows the guy at the door," Heather explained.

"Let's go," Jim said impatiently. "I don't want to stand in line for popcorn."

Gordo couldn't believe it as he followed his cool friends to the front of the line. Sure enough, the guy at the door looked them over, then waved them inside. Not surprisingly, the guy at the door had hair exactly like Gordo's.

"This is amazing," Gordo said as he and his friends walked into the cool, quiet lobby of the movie theater. Gordo couldn't believe that he'd spent his whole life as one of the poor dweebs who had to wait in movie lines. And now—new hair, new style—and his life was totally changed. It was awesome!

Slade gave him a lopsided grin. "You hang with us, you don't have to wait in line."

"Not like those poor suckers out there," Jim added.

Peering through the glass doors, Gordo caught sight of Lucy waiting outside, near the front of the line. Grinning, he waved at her.

But Lucy didn't grin back. Instead, she just looked away, and Gordo felt a weird pang. Suddenly, skipping the line didn't seem so great anymore.

CHAPTER NINE

"How do I look?" Miranda whispered as she and Lizzie walked toward the snack bar at the community pool.

Miranda was wearing an orange halter—the top to a supercute bikini—and an orange sarong with yellow fish on it. Her black hair hung loose, and she had on dark sunglasses.

"For the hundredth time," Lizzie told her. "You look jamtacular." She really does look good, Lizzie thought. "Now, can we please talk about something a little more important? Like—how do *I* look?"

Miranda grinned. "Great. Very *Baywatch*."

Lizzie laughed. She was wearing a red one-piece and had her blond hair tied back in a ponytail. She took a deep breath, trying to quiet the butterflies in her stomach. It was her first official day as assistant lifeguard, and she really wanted to make a good impression.

"Spinach check?" Miranda said, baring her teeth at Lizzie.

"Miranda, there's nothing in your teeth," Lizzie told her friend. "Besides, when was the last time you ate spinach, anyway?"

"Two years ago, my mom managed to sneak it into some lasagna," Miranda admitted.

"Okay, I think you're clear," Lizzie said.

"I just can't help it," Miranda wailed. "I'm supposed to meet the guy of my dreams in"—she checked her watch—"eight minutes, and

I'm totally nervous. What if I can't think of anything to say to him?"

Lizzie looked skeptical. "Miranda, you've been chatting online with the guy for weeks. You'll think of something. And if you feel nervous, just picture him in his underwear."

"Why do people always say that?" Miranda asked, throwing her hands in the air. "That just makes me feel more nervous! I mean, what would I say to some guy in his underwear?"

"Then picture him dressed as your grandma," Lizzie suggested. "Whatever works. Hey, Scott," she said as she and Miranda slid into the stools at the counter across from him.

"Hey, assistant lifeguard," he said with a grin. "Hey, Miranda. What can I get you?"

"How about a smoothie?" Lizzie said.

"Miranda?" Scott asked. "What about you?"

"Oh, nothing," Miranda said, waving her hand. "I'm too nervous."

"You, nervous?" Scott asked, folding his arms across his chest. "Why do I find that hard to believe?"

"I'm just—meeting someone," Miranda said quickly.

"Anyone I know?" Scott asked.

"No . . . actually, I don't even know him," Miranda confessed.

"They met online," Lizzie explained.

Scott nodded, but he didn't say anything. Lizzie couldn't help noticing that his expression had sort of clouded over.

"Anyway, it's really dumb, because we've been chatting online for weeks," Miranda added quickly. "I mean, I know he's really smart, and funny, and sweet—and really, really cute. So what am I nervous about, right?"

Scott nodded, but he seemed far away as he said, "Right." Finally, he cleared his throat and said, "Well, I'd better make that smoothie." He turned to the blender, started adding the ingredients, and turned it on.

"Thanks, Scott," Lizzie said as she shoved a five-dollar bill across the counter at him.

He pushed it back. "Smoothies are free for lifeguards," he said as he poured the drink into a tall glass and added a straw. "And their assistants."

"Really?" Lizzie asked, taking a sip.

Scott nodded.

"Then I guess you'll be seeing a lot more of me," Lizzie told him with a smile.

Scott laughed, but Lizzie noticed that he snuck another look at Miranda before the girls left the snack shack. *Poor Scott,* Lizzie thought. *He's crushin' on Miranda big time.*

"Should I be sitting at a table, or lying on a lounge chair when he comes in?" Miranda asked.

"Lounge chair," Lizzie said. "More casual." Finishing her drink, she tossed the colorful plastic cup into the garbage and glanced at Tate, who was sunning himself in his lifeguard chair. "Okay, I've gotta get to work," Lizzie said. "But if you need me, I'm right here."

Reaching out, Miranda gave her best friend's hand a squeeze. "Thanks so much, Lizzie." Suddenly, her black eyes went wide. "Omigosh, there he is. Hide me."

"Miranda!" Lizzie whispered as her best friend tried to duck behind Lizzie, using her body as a shield. "Knock it off!"

"Miranda?" asked the tall, muscular guy as he walked up to them. He flashed her a brilliant smile. "I'm Blaine."

"Uh," Miranda said. "Uh." She was still squeezing Lizzie's hand.

Oh, man, he *is* brain-meltingly hot, Lizzie had to admit as she gazed up into his piercing green eyes. "Hi, Blaine," she said. "I'm Miranda's friend, Lizzie."

"Hi," Blaine said.

Lizzie kicked Miranda.

"Hi, I'm Miranda," she said suddenly in a voice like a robot.

"Well, it was great meeting you, Blaine," Lizzie said. "I've got to get to work now."

"Oh, I'm sure you don't have to work yet," Miranda said, still crushing Lizzie's fingers in her own.

"Yes, I do," Lizzie said.

"No, you don't," Miranda corrected.

"I really, really do," Lizzie insisted through clenched teeth, prying her fingers free of Miranda's death grip. She finally got loose.

"Have fun!" she said brightly, hurrying away before Miranda could clamp onto her hand again.

Lizzie headed toward the lifeguard's chair as Miranda settled herself onto a lounge chair, smiling nervously at her date. *I'll check in with her later,* Lizzie promised herself. *But I've got to do a little work first.*

"Hey, Tate," Lizzie called up to the gorgeous lifeguard.

Tate looked down at her from behind his mirrored glasses. "Hey."

"I'm Lizzie, the new assistant."

Tate didn't say anything, but she thought she saw him tilt his head forward slightly, which she guessed meant that she should go on. "So, uh, what should I do?" Lizzie asked.

The lifeguard shrugged. "Skim the leaves?"

"Skim the leaves," Lizzie repeated, looking out at the pool. That didn't seem so bad.

There were a few leaves floating near the ladder at the deep end. There was a net like a giant flyswatter hanging up by the side of the lifeguard chair. She would just use that.

"Then maybe test the chlorine level," Tate added. "And check to make sure nothing is sticking in the drains. I think we've got a clog near the shallow end."

"Leaves, chlorine, drains," Lizzie said, nodding.

"Then maybe you could grab me a soda?" Tate suggested. "It's really hot up here."

"You got it," Lizzie said brightly, even though this wasn't exactly the laid-back, fabulous day she'd been expecting. In fact, it seemed kind of like a lot of grunt work.

Oh well, *whatever*, Lizzie thought as she wrapped her fingers around the handle of the skimmer net. I need that money for the demo. And at least I can get close to where

Miranda and Blaine are sitting. Maybe I can overhear something. And help out Miranda, if she needs it.

But Miranda didn't appear to need any help. As Lizzie inched closer, she saw her best friend happily smiling and nodding at Blaine.

"So then I was surfing this massive curl," Blaine said as Lizzie pretended to be totally focused on fishing some dead leaves out of the water. "Most guys wouldn't go near a wave like that, but I'm going semipro next year, so . . ."

Miranda kept on smiling and nodding as Blaine went on.

Say something, Miranda! Lizzie thought. But she couldn't think of a way to just butt in and advise her friend.

Finishing up with the leaves, Lizzie got out the kit to measure the chlorine levels. Since it didn't matter what part of the pool she took the water sample from, she headed back toward the deep end, where Miranda and Blaine were still locked in conversation. Lizzie tiptoed over to them, trying to be inconspicuous.

"So," Miranda said, her voice quavering nervously, "how do you like the Chocolate Rabbits?"

"Actually, I'm allergic to chocolate," Blaine replied. "It gives me hives."

Miranda laughed uncertainly, as though she wasn't sure whether or not he was making a joke. "No—I mean the band, the Chocolate Rabbits? Remember, I told you to download the MP3?"

"Oh, that," Blaine said, waving his hand dismissively. "I never got around to it. Hey, have you seen any of the summer movies? I hear *Nightflame* is awesome."

Miranda glanced at Lizzie, who smiled at her in support, nodding.

"Yeah," Miranda said slowly. "Yeah, I've been meaning to see it. My friend Gordo says it's great."

Okay so that's a total lie, Lizzie thought as she dipped the chlorine tester in the water. Gordo hated that movie. He said it was a mindless action flick with little story, less wit, and nothing visually original. But, whatever, Lizzie told herself. At least Miranda is finally talking.

A whistle blast cut into Lizzie's thoughts. "Lizzie?" Tate called from his chair.

Lizzie leaped to her feet. Only half a day on the job, and someone needed her help! She glanced to where Tate was pointing.

"This little boy dropped his toy dinosaur down there," Tate shouted, pointing to the deepest part of the pool. "Could you dive in and get it for him?"

A skinny little boy with freckles, wearing a

yellow inner tube around his waist gave Lizzie a mean smile and stuck out his tongue at her. *Grrr.* Lizzie gritted her teeth.

Taking a deep breath, Lizzie dove in to the bottom of the deep end. Grabbing the toy dinosaur, she swam to the edge of the pool and handed it to the little boy, who snatched it from her fingers and trotted off without the slightest hint of thanks.

Sighing, Lizzie hauled herself from the pool—only to come face-to-face with Kate.

"Nice save, Lizzie," Kate said, smiling

smugly. She peered at Lizzie over the top of a pair of pink sunglasses. She was wearing full makeup and had pink sparkles in her hair to match her pink sparkly bikini. "I love your hair. The wet look is so in. . . . *Not*!"

Lizzie reached up to touch her hair, which was now plastered to her head. *Oooh*, she fumed as Kate flounced away, if I were a mean person, I'd . . . I'd . . . What *would* I do? After all, I'm only the *assistant* lifeguard. Lizzie narrowed her eyes. I know, she thought. I'd let the chlorine level get so high that Kate's skin would become *seriously* itchy.

Okay, so it's totally lame, but at least being the assistant lifeguard has *some* kind of power, right?

"Here you go!" Lizzie chirped as she handed Tate a tall glass of lemonade. After three days on the job, Lizzie was starting to realize that a big part of being assistant lifeguard was bringing the *real* lifeguard things to drink.

"Thanks, Lizzie," Tate said as he took the lemonade from her. "Listen, would you mind taking care of something for me?"

"Sure," Lizzie told him.

"You see those weeds growing up between the cracks in the pavement at the edge of the kiddie pool? If you could dig them out, that would be great."

Lizzie looked skeptical. "Weeds?" she repeated.

Hey, i'm a lifeguard, not a gardener.

"They're a hazard," Tate explained. "Some little kid could trip over them and fall face-first into the kiddie pool."

Lizzie sighed. "Okay," she said.

"There's a trowel in the swim shack," Tate told her. "Thanks, Lizzie, you're the best!"

Yeah. I'm the best weed digger at the Hillridge community pool.

Once she had headed over to the swim shack and found the trowel, Lizzie started to attack the weeds in the concrete. The sun beat down on her shoulders as she dug. Hey, look on the bright side, Lizzie told herself. If you get too hot, you can always go jump in the pool.

Just think of how happy you'll be when

you're recording in a real studio, with live musicians, Lizzie commanded herself. Before she knew it, she was humming the melody to "You Go, Girl!" as she dug up dandelions.

"Lizzie!" Miranda ran up to her friend, then frowned. "What are you doing?"

"Important lifeguard duty," Lizzie explained. Setting down her trowel, she stood up and faced her friend. "Hey, you look great."

Miranda gave a little twirl, showing off a cool, red-and-black-plaid sundress that was edged in black lace. "I've got another date with Blaine. We're going to a movie. What do you think of the outfit?"

"It's perfect," Lizzie said, "but . . ."

A worry line appeared between Miranda's eyebrows. "But what?"

"I'm just kind of surprised that you're going out with Blaine again," Lizzie said with a shrug. "I thought you said that he was kind of boring." Actually, what Miranda had said was that the in-person Blaine was way cockier and not as smart as he was online. Of course, he was also way cuter.

"I was thinking about that," Miranda said. "You know, I think we were both just nervous meeting each other for the first time. I mean, I was hardly my best self."

"True," Lizzie admitted, remembering how her friend had barely been able to talk to Blaine at first.

"Besides," Miranda said with a brilliant grin, "he's just so hot!"

Lizzie shook her head, smiling. "Well, that outfit is totally jamtacular. You go, girl!"

"Thanks, Lizzie." Miranda giggled and checked her watch. "Listen, I've got to jet. I have to get to the mall—they're having a sale at the Accessories Shack, and I'm thinking this dress needs bangles."

"Wait—you're not going to hang at the pool with me?" Lizzie asked.

Miranda winced. "Can't today—but I'll be here tomorrow. Promise."

"Okay," Lizzie said as Miranda gave her a quick hug and took off.

Sighing, Lizzie turned back to her weeds. So far, Miranda had been way too busy to hang out with her at the pool much—which was kind of a downer. Most of Lizzie's grunt work would have seemed way more bearable if she'd had someone to talk to while she was doing it. But Lizzie understood.

Which would you choose? Go out on a date with Superhunk? Or dig in dirt near a kiddie pool? Thinking, thinking . . .

Lizzie hacked at the weeds for half an hour. It was hot working under the broiling sun. She could feel the beads of perspiration trickling down her face and neck.

i demand to know who thought this job would be no sweat? Whoops . . . that would be *me*.

Lizzie noticed a shadow fall over her. She looked up to find Scott holding out a glass of iced tea. "Thought you might need this," he said.

Lizzie smiled. "Thanks," she said, swiping her damp forehead with the back of her hand. She took the cold drink and eagerly gulped it down.

Scott sat down on the concrete behind her.

"Listen, I wanted to tell you that I'm sorry about this. . . ."

"About what?" Lizzie asked. She stuffed an ice cube in her cheek to help cool her off.

"About this." Scott gestured to the weeds. "I didn't know that being an assistant lifeguard was basically the same as being Chief Grunt."

"Oh, don't worry about it." Lizzie waved her hand. "I like being at the pool. Besides, I really need the money."

"Yeah?" Scott asked with a smile. "What are you going to do with it?"

"Miranda and I are going to record a demo CD," Lizzie said. "We've got a couple of songs, and we're going to enter them in the KZAP contest."

"Oh, yeah," Scott said, nodding. "I mean—" he corrected himself suddenly. "Oh, yeah? I didn't know you guys sang."

Lizzie nodded. "We wrote the songs, too. And Miranda came up with some supercool dance moves."

"That's awesome—so you're working to pay for studio time?"

"That's the idea," Lizzie nodded.

"It can be expensive." Scott stared thoughtfully out over the brilliant blue water.

"Tell me about it," Lizzie agreed.

"Actually," Scott said, "my older brother is a studio musician. He and his friends would probably cut you a deal, if you wanted to work with them."

"Really?" Lizzie asked.

"You'd still have to pay for the studio," Scott said.

"Of course . . . but it would be great if they could record with us!" Lizzie couldn't believe her luck.

"I'll ask him for you," Scott said, grinning.

"I'll tell him that it's his big chance to be part of music history."

"Wow, thanks a lot," Lizzie told him.

Scott picked up the empty iced tea glass and put it on his tray. "So," he said in a very casual voice, "how did Miranda like meeting that guy the other day?"

"Blaine?" Lizzie asked, her heart sinking. "Actually, she's meeting him again tonight."

"Oh," Scott said, his eyes clouding slightly. "That's—great."

"Yeah," Lizzie said flatly. "I guess. . . ." But secretly, Lizzie thought that Blaine wasn't exactly the right guy for Miranda, even if she couldn't admit it.

Scott hesitated for a moment, as if he was about to say something more. But in the end, he just said, "Well, I'll see you around, Lizzie."

"Okay," Lizzie said. "Thanks for the iced tea."

"Anytime," Scott told her.

Lizzie barely had a chance to get back to her weed attack before Gordo walked into the pool area. Lizzie frowned at him. "Gordo, what are you doing?"

"Doing?" he said absently. He had a bright orange yo-yo and was slowly spinning it up and down.

"That's an interesting new hobby you've got going there," Lizzie told him.

And by "interesting," i mean totally *weird*.

"Gordo, seriously, what's up with the kiddie toy?" Lizzie asked.

"I'm conducting a little experiment,"

Gordo admitted, hoisting his video camera. "Now we wait and watch."

"Watch for what?" Lizzie asked, but she didn't have to wait long for her answer. Two guys had just walked into the pool area—both of them were playing with bright orange yo-yos. "Whoa," Lizzie whispered.

"Ah, the power of trend. Just watch," Gordo said, shooting the guys with his video camera. The two started talking to a group of cool kids. The group began clustering around the guys with the yo-yos. One of the dudes in the group insisted on borrowing a yo-yo. He played with it a bit and then got into an argument because he didn't want to give it back.

Lizzie glanced around the pool. A very pretty redheaded girl at the snack shack and a dude near the lifeguard chair were staring with rapt interest at the yo-yos. They moved closer to find out what was up.

Just then, three more kids walked in through the pool gate. All of them had Gordo hair. One of them was playing with a bright orange yo-yo. He was immediately surrounded.

"Gordo, this is seriously freaking me out," Lizzie said. "It's like you've got some kind of Jedi mind control."

"I'm telling you, I do!" Gordo said, his blue eyes wide. "All of a sudden, I'm a trendsetter. Me! With just a few subtle *implications*, people do whatever I do."

"What do you mean by 'implications'?" Lizzie asked.

"Well, take the yo-yos," said Gordo. "I just got a buzz going by implying that some of the hottest stars in Hollywood are now using them for meditation. The orange yo-yo is supposed to be symbolic of the sun. When it goes up and down it signifies the rising and setting of the eternal orb. It's a profound, universal, and philosophical metaphor."

"Oh, Gordo, you've got to be kidding," said Lizzie. "And they fell for that?"

Gordo shrugged. "I told them my cousin is a reporter with *Entertain Me* magazine and there's going to be a big spread on it in the next issue. You know, Lizzie, I could probably make everyone in this town wear tutus around their waists and underpants on their heads if I wanted. That would be great—I bet my film would *definitely* get into the student film festival if I did that."

"Gordo, maybe you should use your powers for good instead of evil," Lizzie suggested, a little freaked out by the gleam in Gordo's eye.

"An interesting idea," Gordo said, pursing his lips thoughtfully. "Maybe I'll try it."

Please try it, Lizzie thought as Gordo continued filming all of the yo-yos around the pool. I don't think I can stand living in a town full of people wearing underpants on their heads.

Just then, Lizzie noticed that one of the guys spinning an orange yo-yo looked familiar. Hey, she realized, that's Blaine. He was standing next to the very pretty redheaded girl from the snack shack—and it sure looked like he was chatting her up. The girl touched his arm and smiled. Blaine laughed at something she said, flashing his ultrawhite teeth.

Lizzie frowned. There was something very wrong about that girl with Blaine, Lizzie thought. Like the fact that she *isn't* Miranda.

CHAPTER TEN

"Hey, Gordo," Lizzie said as she walked up to her friend. He was sitting at a table at the Digital Bean, hunched over a book. "Whatcha reading?"

"Lizzie, I decided to take your advice," Gordo said, putting down the book. "I'm reading *Great Expectations.*"

Lizzie blinked at him. "I never told you to read *Great Expectations,*" she said as she slid into the chair across from his.

"No, but you told me to use my mind-control powers for good," Gordo replied. He gestured to the greater Digital Bean area. "And now, check it out. I just told a few other 'cool' kids how the hottest read this summer from Malibu to Miami is this Dickens masterpiece. I put the word out that everyone who's cool is reading it."

"Omigosh, Gordo," Lizzie said as she looked around. Sure enough, at least half of the kids at the Bean were either carrying or reading a copy of *Great Expectations.* "This puts the 'eek' in 'freaky,'" Lizzie whispered.

"I'm going to make sure that all of these trend victims go to college," Gordo said. He stroked his chin. "I wonder how I can make advanced calculus seem cool?"

"Well, at least you aren't playing with that orange yo-yo anymore," Lizzie said, smiling. She was really happy to be hanging with him.

Gordo had been so busy with his film project, and Lizzie with the pool, that it had been a while since they just chilled out together.

"Hey, that reminds me," Gordo said, "do you want to go to Shango Tango tonight? I got passes from a kid in film class—I thought I'd ask Miranda, too."

"I'm there," Lizzie said as she settled into her chair. Shango Tango was the hottest dance club in town—they played all of the newest music. "I'm sure Miranda would love to go, too." If she isn't busy with Blaine, she added mentally.

Just then—almost as though she had mentally paged him—Blaine walked into the Digital Bean. Lizzie couldn't help smiling as she noticed that he was carrying a copy of *Great Expectations.* But a moment later, a girl with long, curly brown hair walked in behind him and took his hand. The two of them sat down at the counter.

"What's wrong?" Gordo asked, noticing Lizzie's wide-eyed expression.

"You see that guy at the counter?" Lizzie asked. "With the copy of *Great Expectations*?"

"Which one?" Gordo asked, following Lizzie's gaze.

"The one on the end, with the curly-haired girl."

"Yeah."

"That's Blaine," Lizzie whispered.

Gordo stared at her. "Miranda's Blaine? The Internet guy?"

Lizzie nodded.

"Uh, Lizzie, is it just me, or does it look like he's on a date with some other girl?" Gordo asked as Blaine tucked a stray curl behind the girl's ear.

"It isn't just you," Lizzie admitted.

"Hmm . . . interesting."

"What?" Lizzie asked, glaring at Gordo.

He shrugged. "It's just . . . the Hillridge Central chat room is used by a bunch of different schools. I guess, if you wanted to, you could date a lot of different girls—and there's really no way they'd ever find out about it."

"Gordo! Do you think that's what he's doing?" Lizzie asked, worried.

Gordo turned slightly pale. "I hope not." But his eyes said, *sure looks like it, though.*

They both glanced at Blaine.

"Do you think we should tell Miranda?" Lizzie whispered.

"We?" Gordo repeated. "Lizzie, you know I'm no good at talking about girl stuff."

Lizzie sighed. "Does that mean that you think *I* should tell her?"

"I think you have to," Gordo said, nodding. "Before she gets really into this guy."

An image of Miranda's giddy smile as she

talked about her perfect Internet boy flashed through Lizzie's mind. "Too late."

Gordo hauled himself out of his chair. "Come on," he said, poking Lizzie in the arm. "I'll walk you to Miranda's house."

"And give me a pep talk on the way?" Lizzie asked hopefully. She really didn't want to tell Miranda the truth about Blaine—she knew it was going to hurt, bad.

"It's the least I can do," Gordo said.

Just as Lizzie stood up to leave, there was some sort of commotion at the entrance to the Digital Bean. A crowd of people had clustered around someone, and the whole group was working its way into the cybercafé.

"Please, everyone!" shouted a familiar voice. "Please—you're disturbing my concentration!"

A hush fell over the crowd.

What in the—? Lizzie elbowed her way

through the crowd just in time to hear Matt announce, "My assistant, Lanny, is scheduling appointments. But I have to warn you, there's a six-week waiting list."

Lanny stood there, clipboard in hand, as the kids lined up to put their names on the list.

"Matt," Lizzie demanded, "what do you think you're doing?"

"Lizzie," Matt said patiently, "I know you're my sister, but if you want a haircut, you're going to have to schedule an appointment like everyone else."

Lizzie looked over at Gordo, who shrugged.

"I've got an appointment!" shrieked a girl with a long dark ponytail. "See you in September!" she told Matt happily, practically skipping out of the café.

"It means so much to bring happiness to the world," Matt murmured as he watched her go. "Well!" he said brightly, turning to Lizzie. "See you guys later." He walked over to the counter to place his order. Lanny and the knot of haircut customers trailed after him.

Lizzie rolled her eyes. "Is it just me, or are things getting seriously weird around here?"

"Hey, sweetie," Mrs. McGuire said as Lizzie walked into the kitchen.

"Hey," Lizzie said listlessly, flopping onto a stool at the kitchen island.

"Hmm, that didn't sound too happy," Lizzie's mom said as she chopped up some veggies for a salad. Lizzie's dad was already out on the deck, grilling up salmon steaks for dinner. Even though Lizzie's stomach growled at the sight of one of her favorite meals, she just didn't feel like eating. She was too worried about Miranda.

When Lizzie and Gordo had arrived at Miranda's house, her mom told them that Miranda had just left for the mall. She wanted to get her nails done because she was supposed to meet Blaine that evening. So they just left the message about Gordo's getting passes to Shango Tango—even though Lizzie knew Miranda would never come, now that she was spending the evening with Blaine. Then Lizzie and Gordo headed home.

It just seems so unfair, Lizzie thought miserably. Why can't things turn out right, for once?

"Is everything okay?" Mrs. McGuire asked.

"Mom, I kind of have this problem," Lizzie confessed.

Mrs. McGuire put down her knife. "What is it?"

"Well, I have this friend . . ."

"A *friend*, hmm?" Lizzie's mom repeated

with a knowing look over the top of her black-framed glasses.

Lizzie rolled her eyes. "It's not *me*," she said. "Jeez, Mom, sometimes my friends really do have problems, you know."

"Oh, sorry."

Lizzie fidgeted on her stool. "So I have this friend, and she met this guy online . . ."

"Lizzie!" Mrs. McGuire's eyes flashed with alarm. "You know you have to be very careful when you're talking to people online. They could be dangerous—"

"Mom," Lizzie said, interrupting her mother. "It's okay. First of all, she met the guy in a closed, monitored middle-school chat room. Second, when she finally met him in person, she did it in public. And third, it's *not me*, remember?"

Lizzie's mother sighed. "Okay." She folded her arms across her chest, then flapped one hand at Lizzie. "Go on."

"So, anyway, my friend met this guy, and she really likes him." Lizzie stopped, thinking about how Miranda had gone on and on about Blaine that afternoon. True, she'd said that they hadn't talked much on their date. But he had sent her a really funny e-mail afterward that had totally cracked her up. "But I've seen the guy around with a couple of different girls. And I'm worried he's going to break her heart."

"Oh, no," Lizzie's mom said, shaking her

head. "So, now you have to figure out whether to tell Miranda what you saw or keep it to yourself."

"I never said it was Miranda," Lizzie said quickly.

"Lizzie, please." Mrs. McGuire shook her head. "You don't have to be a genius to figure that one out."

Whoa, did i miss something? Like, where is my mother hiding the detective who's finally giving her a clue?

"So what am I going to do?" Lizzie asked. "Either way, she could get really hurt."

"Well," Lizzie's mother said slowly, getting back to her chopping, "are you sure this guy was out on *dates* with these girls? I mean, it could be innocent. You might have seen him with cousins, family members, or other friends. Miranda and Gordo are just friends and they spend time together, right?"

Lizzie bit her lip. "I guess it's *possible*," she admitted.

"Well, you have to be careful when you accuse people of things, Lizzie. And there's one other thing you haven't thought of," said Mrs. McGuire.

"What's that?" asked Lizzie.

"It's possible Miranda already knows."

"Knows? Knows what?" asked Lizzie.

"This boy may have already mentioned to Miranda that he's dating other girls," said her mother. "That he isn't ready to go steady—or whatever you kids call it these days."

Lizzie sighed. She realized that her mother had a point. And she also realized that all her worries could be cleared up by one *honest* conversation with her best friend.

Lizzie walked toward the phone but then stopped herself. This is pretty sensitive stuff, she thought. It might turn out to be no big deal to Miranda, or it could turn out to be a really big deal and really bad news. But it for sure isn't the kind of news anyone should be told over the phone, Lizzie decided. I'll just have to wait until the next time we have some alone time together.

Just then, the doorbell rang.

"I'll get it," Lizzie said, drooping out of her chair. She dragged herself to the front door and yanked it open. "Oh, hello, Mrs. Walker." Lizzie was actually surprised to see their sour-faced neighbor from down the street. Mrs. Walker was an older lady with stiff white hair, who had the most beautiful flower beds in town. She sat on her porch with her dog and never, ever said hello to any of the neighbors.

Mrs. Walker scowled. "Is your mother at home?" she demanded in a tight little voice.

"Hello, Mrs. Walker," Mrs. McGuire said, appearing behind Lizzie.

"Look what that boy of yours did to my dog!" Mrs. Walker pointed at her feet, where a small white poodle sat, looking up at Lizzie with a silly grin on his face. The dog had a Mohawk, and someone had shaved his legs, leaving small fur pom-poms at his feet and at the tip of his tail, which were dyed green.

Lizzie had to stifle a laugh.

Oh, worm-boy! i'd like to see how you're going to squirm your way out of this one!

Mrs. McGuire turned pale. "Matt!" she shouted.

Matt came running. "Oh, hi, Mrs. Walker. Hey, Muffin!" The toy poodle hurried over to Matt, green tail wagging furiously. Matt bent down to pat the dog on the Mohawk. "How do you like his haircut?" Matt asked. "No charge."

"No *charge*?" Mrs. Walker growled. "My poor Muffin looks like he belongs in the circus!"

Matt looked horrified. "Muffin is my masterpiece!"

"You McGuires just let that boy run wild!" Mrs. Walker spat at Lizzie's mother. "You'd better see that he's punished, or I'll—"

"Oh, I can assure you that he'll be punished, Mrs. Walker," Mrs. McGuire said. "My husband and I will handle this."

Mrs. Walker's mouth clamped shut. She

narrowed her eyes at Matt and shouted, "You stay away from Muffin!" Then she snapped her fingers, and Muffin bounded into her arms. A minute later, they were striding down the front walk.

Matt shook his head. "Some people just don't appreciate a free haircut."

"Matt," Mrs. McGuire said, folding her arms across her chest. "I know that you love to cut hair, but you can't just go around trimming the neighbors' dogs without their permission."

"But Muffin liked it, Mom!" Matt wailed.

"But her owner *didn't*," Lizzie pointed out. "That poodle looks like it should be playing drums in a punk band."

"Quiet, both of you." Mrs. McGuire held up a hand. "Matt, you're grounded for a week. And from now on, you'd better stick to human hair," she added over Matt's squeak of protest.

At last! Matt's crazy behavior finally gets punished! The first glimmer of hope that the world cannot stay insane forever.

"And, Mom, *please* make him promise to stick to *paying* customers," Lizzie demanded. The past few days, Matt had been eyeing her hair in a way she did *not* like.

"Fine," Matt snapped. "From now on, I'll only cut the hair of people who actually ask for it. But I'm warning you, this could have a serious effect on my creativity."

We should be so lucky.

CHAPTER ELEVEN

"This is awesome, Gordo," Lizzie said as she looked around the cool teen dance club, Shango Tango. It was the hottest spot in town, and the place was definitely hopping tonight. The cavernous room was dark, lit only with black lights, which made the elaborate neon murals on the wall glow strangely. Anything white appeared a funky glowing lavender color—like Miranda's halter and Gordo's teeth.

"I can't believe we got to skip the line," Lizzie continued, "the place is packed." The dance floor was swarming with kids who were grooving to the hip-hop beats spun by the live DJ. "And I'm so glad that you could come along, Miranda!"

Blaine had had to cancel their date at the last minute because he said his grandmother had just gone into the hospital and his family had to visit her.

Actually, Lizzie was glad that Blaine had canceled on Miranda. Now Lizzie could finally talk to her best friend about Blaine—and find out what kind of understanding she had with him about seeing other girls.

Lizzie had it all figured out. Once she knew where Miranda stood with Blaine, then she could very gently mention that she'd seen him around with other girls. She planned to tell Miranda that she honestly didn't know if the girls were cousins or just friends or whatever. But she'd certainly suggest that Miranda talk to Blaine about it and find out. That is, if she didn't know already.

"Yeah," Miranda agreed as she took a sip of her drink. "I'm glad I'm here. This music is jamtacular, and I love this strawberry juice." Shango Tango had a crazy menu of fruit juices—everything from pineapple to papaya—and specialty sodas, like celery and rhubarb. "Do you think I could get another one?"

Gordo waved his hand. "Go ahead," he said smoothly as he taped the scene with his video camera. "They're on the house. I know the guy at the counter."

"Then I'm definitely going back," Miranda declared. "Lizzie?"

"I'm good," Lizzie said, holding up her kiwi juice.

Miranda scurried off for a refill.

"Yo, Gordo!" shouted a guy from the dance floor. He had cool blue tips in his hair.

"Peace!" Gordo shouted.

Lizzie couldn't believe the transformation in her fashion-challenged friend. With his black cargo pants, green funky-patterned shirt, green tinted sunglasses, and that cool haircut, the guy Kate Sanders liked to call "Gordork" was now Mr. Cool.

Who knew Gordo could look so at home at Shango Tango? Lizzie thought as she watched her friend capture the teen scene on film. *But he was fitting right in. In fact, it almost seems like he owns the place.*

Just then, Slade came over and slapped Gordo on the shoulder. "Gordo, my man!" he cried. "We've been waiting for you to get here."

"Hey, Slade," said Gordo, smoothly giving

him a three-part fist-knocking handshake. "You remember my friend, Lizzie."

"Hi," Lizzie said, and Slade nodded.

"So, where are the funky beats you promised us?" Slade asked, turning back to Gordo.

"Got 'em right here," Gordo said, slapping a pocket on the side of his leg. "*Imported*, you know. From Europe."

"*Imported*," repeated Slade, nodding his head seriously. "Dude, you are so connected."

"I'm going to wait until the place really heats up," said Gordo, "then I'll have Tucker unleash them on the crowd."

Lizzie lifted an eyebrow. Did Gordo mean Tucker Felix? She was the DJ for Shango Tango—one of the hottest in town. Lizzie glanced up at the booth where an older girl with long pink dreadlocks spun the music. Was it really possible that Gordo knew her?

"Excellent." Slade grinned, then slapped

Gordo on the back again. "I'll let my peeps know you've got some cool new *imported* stuff coming. That'll get the crowd buzzing."

"Dig it," Gordo said.

Slade held out a fist and the two knocked knuckles again. "Dig it," Slade repeated. "Cool."

Lizzie gave Gordo a dubious look. "*Dig it*?" she repeated, once Slade was out of earshot.

Gordo shrugged. "Eh, I just threw that out there to see if it would catch on. I'm planning to revive lots of old words and phrases, like 'twenty-three skidoo,' and 'mod.'"

"Just how far do you think you can take this being cool thing, Gordo?" Lizzie asked.

"As far as it will go," Gordo replied.

"You will not believe this," Miranda said as she walked up to them. "When I told the guy at the snack bar that I knew Gordo, not only did he give me the strawberry juice for free, but he threw in a bag of these ultraspicy pretzels! Who wants one?" Miranda held out the bag.

"Hi, Gordo!" A heavyset girl walked up to them. She had big, weird, cherry red, rimmed glasses and dark hair cut in a strange Cleopatra style. Her sleeveless dress looked like something people wore in the sixties. The fabric was faded, like she'd picked it up in a thrift shop, and the hemline fell past her knees, which put it about two feet below every other skirt hemline in the dance club.

"Hey, Lucy," Gordo said. "These are my friends Miranda and Lizzie. Lucy's in my film class."

"Oh, hi!" Lucy waved. "I've heard all about you guys."

Miranda held out her bag. "Want a pretzel?"

"Sure." Lucy took one. "Wow! Spice-a-rino! You could put gas companies out of business with that heat!"

Lizzie laughed—and found herself wondering what was up with Lucy. The girl didn't look like she fit in with the superslick crowd Gordo had been hanging with, but Lizzie liked her right away. For one thing, she was funny. And for another, there was something really genuine about her smile.

"Aren't they good?" Miranda asked, her mouth full of pretzel. "Have another. They're on the house. Gordo knows the snack guy."

"Gordo seems to know everybody," Lucy said, taking another pretzel. "So, Gordo, how did you like the movie the other day? We both went to see *D.O.A.* at the Noir Festival," she explained to Lizzie and Miranda.

"I thought it was great," Gordo said. "Especially the ending."

"Oh, yeah," Lucy agreed, her eyes glowing warmly. "I love the way that was shot. But for me, the best part was—"

"Gordo?" An older girl with a nose ring, hot-pink dreadlocks, low riders, and a belly shirt had just tapped Gordo on the shoulder. Lizzie gaped at her. It was Tucker Felix—the DJ! She had just come right up to Gordo, like it was no big deal.

"Oh, hey, Tucker," Gordo said.

"I hear you have some fresh beats for me. *Imported.* Want to come up to the booth and give them a spin?"

"Let's do it," Gordo said, pulling the CD from his side pocket. "I'll see you later, you guys," he said over his shoulder to Lizzie, Miranda, and Lucy.

"Bye!" Miranda said through chews of her pretzel.

"Yeah," Lucy said softly. "See you." Lizzie

thought that her voice sounded a little disappointed. "Well, I've got to get back to my friends. It was nice meeting you."

"You, too," Lizzie said sincerely. "See you!"

Lucy gave a little wave and took off.

"She seems cool," Miranda said as she watched her go.

"Yeah," Lizzie agreed. There was something about Lucy that was really different. She was cool like the way Gordo used to be, before he became the big trendsetting genius.

Just then, the music stopped. There was a moment of silence, then Gordo's voice boomed over the microphone. "Check it out—the hot new *imported* sound out of Europe! Give it up for Boryslaw's Polish Wonder!" A moment later, the bouncy beat of polka music poured from the speakers.

For a moment, nobody moved.

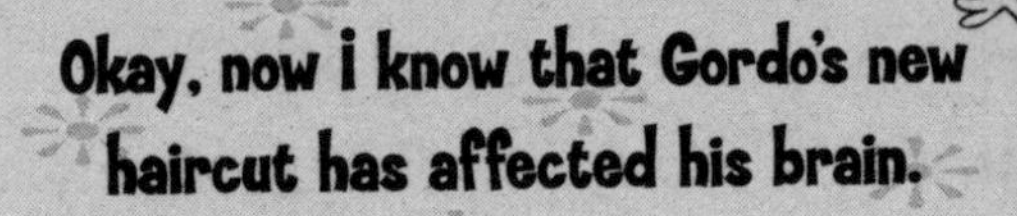

"Everybody polka!" Gordo shouted into the microphone.

Suddenly, a huge cheer rose from the dance floor, and everyone started bopping to the bouncy rhythm. A moment later, the floor was alive with people jumping and dancing to *accordion* music!

Miranda's jaw was hanging open as she watched the action on the dance floor. "What's going on?" she asked.

"I have no idea," Lizzie admitted as she watched the crowd go wild. "I only know one thing—Gordo has *way* too much power."

* * *

"I'm so glad that's over," Miranda said twenty minutes later, once the polka music had mercifully come to an end.

Tucker had finally mixed in some trendy hip-hop.

"This looks like our chance to hit the dance floor," Lizzie suggested. Bizarrely, once the polka music was over, a lot of people had stopped dancing. For the first time all night, there was a little space to move.

"Great idea." Miranda put down her drink.

Gordo was still up in the DJ booth, chatting with Tucker, so Lizzie led the way to the dance floor. But just as she reached the edge, she stopped in her tracks.

Blaine was at the center of the floor, with yet another girl. This one was wearing a tight black miniskirt and red tank top, and she had a mass of blond curls. Lizzie knew two things in that moment: (1) Blaine had lied to

Miranda about visiting his grandmother in the hospital tonight, which meant he couldn't have been honest with her about seeing other girls; and (2) the girl he was dancing with was *not* his sister or his cousin—because the girl was Kate Sanders!

"You know what?" Lizzie said quickly, whipping around. "I just realized that I don't want to dance."

"What?" Miranda asked in confusion. "It was your idea."

"That's true," Lizzie admitted, "but, you know, I think I'm really thirsty. Let's go get some strawberry juice."

"First of all, you're allergic to strawberries, remember?" Miranda said. "Second of all, if I have any more juice, I'll explode." Miranda moved past Lizzie.

"Come on, Miranda, I'm really thirsty," Lizzie improvised.

"So go get the juice and I'll meet you on the dance floor," Miranda replied. "I don't want to wait until they're playing that polka music again."

Over Miranda's shoulder, Lizzie saw Blaine give Kate a kiss. Miranda started to turn in that direction, but Lizzie yanked her back. "Ow!" Lizzie cried. "I think I have a cramp in my leg!"

"You *think* you have a cramp in your leg?" Miranda repeated. "No offense, Lizzie, but you're acting really weird." Then she turned toward the dance floor, and that's when she saw it—the kiss. Kate and Blaine.

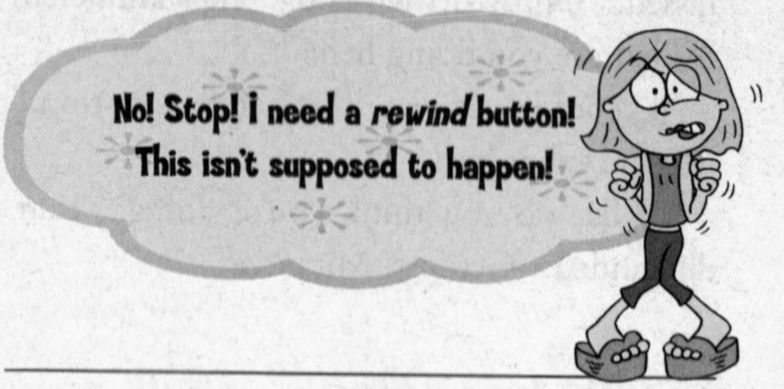

"Miranda, I—" Lizzie bit back the words. The expression on Miranda's face was too horrible. Heartbreak was stamped across her features. "Miranda," Lizzie said softly, touching her friend's arm.

But in the next moment, Miranda was walking forward. She hadn't seemed to hear Lizzie—she was just moving toward Blaine and Kate, her fists balled with fury.

"Miranda!" Lizzie shouted, but it was no use.

"Hey!" Miranda shouted, striding right up to Blaine and poking him in the shoulder.

Blaine looked up, surprised and embarrassed. "Oh, M-M-Miranda," he stammered. "What are you doing here?"

"I could ask *you* the same question," Miranda shot back.

"What do you think you're doing?" Kate demanded. "Get lost, Miranda."

Miranda ignored her. "So—I'm glad to see that your grandmother is feeling better," she snapped at Blaine, her arms folded across her chest.

"Oh, uh, yeah," Blaine lied just as the music switched to a slow song.

"What are you talking about?" Kate demanded.

Miranda wheeled to face her. "Blaine and I were supposed to go out tonight," she explained. "But his grandmother went into the hospital. So we're going out tomorrow instead. Isn't that right, Blaine?"

Kate gave Blaine a raised-eyebrow look.

"Well, uh, you know . . ." Blaine hedged.

"Whatever happened to 'you're the most wonderful girl I've ever met'?" Miranda demanded. "What about 'you're the only one for me'?"

"What?" Kate shrieked, giving her blond

curls a toss. "You said the same thing to me!" She shoved Blaine's shoulder.

"Hey!" Just then, a very pretty red-haired girl elbowed her way through the crowd that had gathered around Blaine, Miranda, and Kate. The music played on, but nobody was dancing. "What are you doing to my boyfriend?" the redhead shouted.

"*Your* boyfriend?" Kate demanded. "He's mine!"

"You wish!" the redhead said.

"Just how many girls are you dating, Blaine?" Miranda demanded.

"Yeah!" shouted a voice, and a tall, slender African American girl stepped out of the crowd. "Just how many of us are there, *Blaine*?"

"Well, uh—you know . . ." Blaine looked around, his voice still smooth. "There's a very simple explanation. You see. . . ." With a quick move, he darted toward the exit.

"You'd *better* run!" shouted the redhead, as she, Kate, and half the girls in Shango Tango took off after him, and Miranda found herself standing alone at the center of the dance floor.

Miranda stared after the departing crowd, unbelieving. Her perfect guy . . . gone.

A hand rested on her shoulder. "I'm sorry," Lizzie said.

Miranda shook her head. "I believed him," she whispered. "He said I was the only one."

"I'm so sorry," Lizzie said again.

"Don't be," Miranda told her. "It's not like it's your fault. You didn't know."

Wincing, Lizzie looked at the ground.

"What?" Miranda asked, peering into her friend's face.

Lizzie pressed her lips together.

"What? Are you saying you *did* know?" Miranda's voice took on a steely edge.

"No, I didn't," Lizzie said quickly. "That is, I wasn't sure. I mean, I was going to tell you this afternoon. I even went to your house, but you were at the mall. The thing is . . . I had seen Blaine with a couple of other girls, but I was hoping that maybe they were just friends, or cousins, or maybe he had let you know that he was seeing other girls. That it was really okay with you—"

Lizzie closed her eyes.

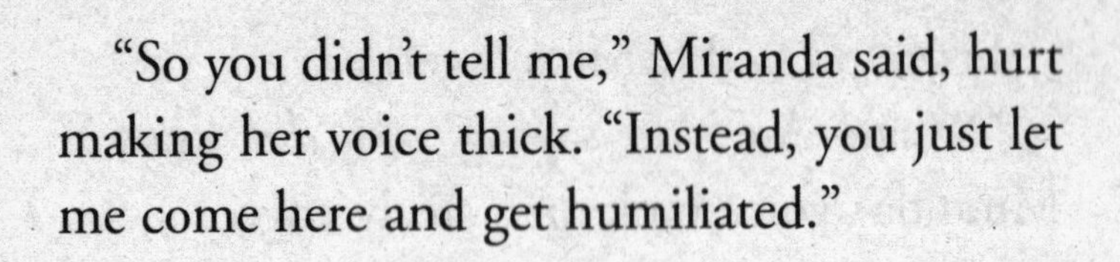

"So you didn't tell me," Miranda said, hurt making her voice thick. "Instead, you just let me come here and get humiliated."

"I didn't want to hurt you," Lizzie protested. "I was waiting for the right time to break it to you."

"Well, time's up, Lizzie," Miranda said bitterly. With an icy glare, she turned and stalked out of the club.

"Miranda!" Lizzie shouted after her friend. "I didn't mean—"

But it was too late. Miranda was already out the door.

"Hey," Gordo said, tapping Lizzie on the shoulder. "Where did Miranda go? What's going on?"

Lizzie shook her head. "Honestly, Gordo," she said with a sigh, "you don't want to know."

CHAPTER TWELVE

"Hey, Lucy," Gordo said as he slipped into the folding chair next to hers.

Lucy looked at him coolly. "Hello," she said, then looked down at her notebook.

"So," Gordo said. "We'll get to see everyone's movies today."

Lucy just shrugged and stared out at the front of the classroom.

"I already asked Hathaway if I could go first," Gordo went on. "I'm fairly confident that my documentary will be chosen for the student film festival. . . . Hey, Camy!" Gordo called brightly as a girl in the front row waved to him. "I really think you're going to like it."

"Why are you talking to me?" Lucy asked suddenly.

Gordo gaped at her. "What? What do you mean?"

"I mean, why are you talking to me all of a sudden?" Lucy repeated, stabbing at her notebook with the tip of her pen. "You've been blowing me off for the past few weeks to hang with your cool friends. Maybe you'd better go sit with them." Her eyes were bright with angry tears. "In case you hadn't noticed, Gordo, I'm not exactly popular material."

"Lucy, I—"

"All right, students of film," Hathaway said as he walked into the classroom. "Today is our last meeting, and we will be watching the final projects—your own student films. The first one will be . . ." Hathaway looked down at the tape in his hand. *Undercover Nerd*, by David Gordon."

Gordo snuck a sideways look at Lucy as Hathaway popped the tape into the VCR and pressed PLAY. A huge cheer went up from the class when Gordo's name appeared in the opening credits. The popular kids in the front row—all of them with Gordo hair—went wild. But Gordo didn't feel happy. Lucy seemed really upset.

The tape started to roll—it was Gordo on the first day of class, dressed in his typical Gordo oversize vintage shirt and discount store cargo pants, long curls flopping over his eyes. No one except Lucy paid any attention to him.

"Ah, the nerd," Gordo's voice narrated over the action, "also known as the invisible man, the bottom of the food chain. With his unfashionable clothes and hair, nobody pays him any mind."

But in the next scene, everything changed. Gordo walked into class with his new haircut and his Hollywood-cool clothes, and he was almost immediately mobbed by people. "With a simple style change, the nerd comes out of his cocoon, like a butterfly," Gordo's voice went on.

A little stab of pride shot through Gordo as he watched the movie. It was fun to see the "cool" kids fawning all over him once his look changed, and he thought he had done a good job with the narration. But, as he watched the movie, his pride dried up and disappeared—because in the corner of the shot, Gordo could see a girl with long blond hair elbow Lucy out of the way to talk to him. There was just enough time to see the look of hurt that crossed Lucy's face before she sat down. He had watched this footage a hundred times, but he'd never noticed that before.

A hush fell over the class as the film showed first one, then two, then five of the students turning into Gordo clones. Nobody was laughing or cheering anymore.

Next up was the scene in which Gordo cut the line at the Film Noir Festival.

"My friends and I have been waiting in line for two hours," Lucy said onscreen.

"But the cool need not wait," Gordo's voice narrated as the movie showed him, Slade, and their friends heading to the front of the line. "A special space is reserved for those at the top of the heap."

Gordo could feel Lucy looking at him, but he didn't dare look back. He hadn't realized how awful that sounded before he put it in the movie. And he had also never thought about the fact that he had completely blown Lucy off at the festival.

There were scenes of Gordo playing with his yo-yo, and scenes of everyone reading the same "hot" summer book. There was even a shot of Hathaway reading *Great Expectations.*

"I've always loved Dickens," Hathaway said defensively into the camera.

At the front of the classroom, the real, live Hathaway shifted awkwardly as a titter rippled through the class.

Finally, there was the scene in Shango Tango, where everyone got down to polka music. Slade was bopping around madly to the wailing accordion.

"The cool possess a certain kind of mind control," Gordo's voice said onscreen. "But is anything really cool just because everyone else is doing it? What's cooler: doing what other people do? Or doing what you like because you've discovered it uniquely for yourself?"

The room was silent as the film ended and the lights went up.

Gordo looked around the room. He felt a pang as he saw the looks of embarrassment on his classmates' faces. He hadn't meant to hurt so many feelings.

"Uh, very interesting," Hathaway said finally. "A good film tells the truth—and that can make us very uncomfortable." He cleared his throat, his face red with embarrassment. "Nice work, Mr. Gordon. The next film is—"

"No," Gordo said, standing up. "Wait."

Hathaway looked up at him. "Yes?"

Gordo took a deep breath. He had to give his teacher credit—Hathaway was being very objective and fair toward his film.

"Listen," Gordo told the class, "I'm sorry if I hurt anyone's feelings. All I wanted to do was make a film about how people changed around me when I looked different. About how nerds are ignored simply because of the way they look. After all . . . I never changed. Only my hair and my clothes did." Gordo shrugged. "All I'm saying is that sometimes people make snap judgments about others and maybe they should be more sensitive, open their eyes, try to look a little deeper."

The room was totally quiet as Gordo finished. "And if I'm totally honest here, I have to admit that I wasn't very sensitive myself." He looked down at his friend. "Lucy, I didn't realize what a jerk I was being. How I hurt your feelings. I'm sorry."

Lucy looked up at him, her dark eyes shining. "It's okay," she said in a soft voice.

Gordo sat back in his chair and quietly added, "I can't believe that I let a movie become more important than a friend."

A slow grin spread across Lucy's face.

"Well," she said, "at least it was a good movie."

"So," Gordo said, "what are you doing after class? Do you want to check out the latest film at the Noir Festival?"

Lucy shrugged. "I'll have to check my schedule."

Gordo could tell that she was joking. He smiled. He guessed his film wouldn't be entered in the student film festival, after all. But he could live with that.

In the end, Gordo knew that making a real movie didn't matter as much as making a real friend.

Lizzie fished a few soggy leaves from the deep end of the pool. So far today, Tate had asked her to reorganize the kickboards by size, untangle the water polo net, check all of the pool's water wings for leaks, and fetch him three smoothies.

"Hey, Lizzie," Tate called from his seat on the lifeguard chair, "could you bring me some more sunscreen?"

Lizzie narrowed her eyes at him. The sunscreen was sitting at the foot of his chair. All he had to do was climb down to get it—it wasn't that hard. But, of course, it's harder than bossing around your lackey, Lizzie thought as she set her skimmer net back in the rack and trudged over to the lifeguard chair. "Here you go," Lizzie said as she handed the bottle up to Tate.

"So," Tate said, looking down at her through his mirrored shades, "I guess you're sad to be leaving us."

"Yeah," Lizzie lied. Actually, she couldn't have been happier that today was her last shift at the pool. Tate had turned out to be seriously bossy, for one thing. And for another, Miranda had been so busy with Blaine that she hadn't hung out at the pool half as much as she had promised.

At least I made a bundle of money for our demo, Lizzie thought miserably—*not that it's going to help much, now that Miranda isn't even talking to me. So I guess our whole dream of winning the contest is over. All of this stupid grunt work . . . for nothing.*

"Well, maybe you'll be back next year," Tate said. "I could always use an assistant." The sun gleamed off of his shades, and Lizzie realized that Tate had spent the whole summer bossing her around . . . and she still had no idea what color his eyes were.

"Maybe so," Lizzie said vaguely.

Yeah, right. If I come back, it'll be as a lifeguard, not an assistant. That way, I can be the one doing the bossing around here.

Lizzie tramped over to the rack that held the skimmer net. But just as she reached for it, her eyes fell on a figure at the pool gate. Black hair, orange sarong—it was Miranda. Before she even had time to remember that they were in a fight, Lizzie lifted her hand and waved.

Miranda waved back. "Hey, Lizzie," she said tentatively as she walked over.

"Hey." Lizzie bit her lip. She wasn't sure whether her best friend was there to yell at her, or to make up. But Lizzie decided to plunge in with her apology, anyway. "Listen, Miranda, I am so sorry that I didn't tell you about Blaine. It's just that you liked him so much, and I just really wasn't sure of anything—"

Miranda held up a hand. "It's okay," she said, shaking her head. "I'm the one who should be sorry."

Lizzie took a deep, relieved breath.

"I know you were just trying to protect me," Miranda went on. "And I'm sorry I got so mad. I was just really, really disappointed . . . about Blaine." She swallowed hard, and Lizzie reached for her hand. Miranda squeezed her fingers.

"Me, too," Lizzie admitted. "I know he was your dream guy."

Miranda scoffed. "More like a nightmare," she corrected.

"But there's a Mister Right Guy still out there for you somewhere," Lizzie went on. "You know that, don't you?"

"Yeah," Miranda admitted. "I guess next time, I'll just be a little more skeptical of anyone I meet online."

"So . . . I guess this means we're friends again?" Lizzie asked with a smile.

"Of course," Miranda said, wrapping her in a hug. "Best friends. Forever. One fight could never change that."

"Well, I'm glad to hear it," Lizzie said, pulling back to look her friend in the eye, "because I've got all of this money from working like a dog for the past few weeks. . . ."

"And there's another thing I should

apologize about," Miranda went on. "I realized that I had promised to hang out with you while you worked. And I barely showed up at all. I guess I had a bad case of Blaine Brain."

it's amazing how many iQ points you can lose just by thinking about a guy.

"It's okay," Lizzie told her friend, but secretly Lizzie was really glad that Miranda said she was sorry. "So—are we going to make this demo, or what?"

"Well," Miranda said, the corners of her eyes crinkling into a smile, "I'm free tomorrow."

"And it just so happens that I don't have to work—" Lizzie said.

"Let's do it!"

"Hey, Miranda," Scott said as he walked up to the two girls. "Haven't seen you around lately."

"Yeah," Miranda said with a smile as she and Lizzie wrapped their arms around each other's shoulders, "I guess I've been busy. But then I got a clue." She and Lizzie cracked up.

"Listen, Lizzie, I talked to my brother," Scott said. "Todd said that he and his band would record with you guys for half price, since you're a friend."

"That's great!" Lizzie beamed as she and Miranda high-fived.

"We're going to be stars!" Miranda chimed in.

Scott smiled shyly. "You're already stars."

"Aww." Miranda punched him in the arm. "Scott, you're always so sweet."

"Yeah, well . . ." Scott dug a slip of paper

out of the breast pocket of his hideous orange shirt. "Here's the address of the studio. Can you make it tomorrow at around ten?"

"Could this be more perfect?" Lizzie asked as she took the number from Scott.

"Only if we win the contest," Miranda said.

"Oh, you'll win," Scott said confidently.

"You've never even heard us sing!" Miranda protested.

Scott shrugged and flushed a little. "Well—what can I say? I'm good at spotting talent."

Let's hope that's true, Lizzie thought as she looked down at the address in her hand. KZAP, here we come!

Lizzie and Miranda arrived fifteen minutes early for their recording session the next day.

"Are you sure this is it?" Miranda asked as

she looked up at the large warehouse-style building.

"It's the right address," Lizzie said uncertainly. Pushing open the door, she and Miranda stepped into an elegant lobby, complete with leather couches and framed gold mirrors on the wall.

"Looks a lot better from the inside," Miranda said.

"Miranda!" someone called. "Lizzie!"

Lizzie turned to see a supercute guy in a soft green polo shirt and jeans walking toward them. His brown hair shagged around his ears in a cool-but-not-trying-to-be-cool way. She didn't recognize him for a full minute—until he smiled. "Scott?" Lizzie said.

it's amazing what removing a dorky orange uniform can do for a guy's style.

"Hey!" Scott's eyes twinkled as he looked at Miranda. "It's cool that you're here early. Why don't you come meet the band?"

Scott led them to one of the studios and introduced them to his brother, Todd, who played bass. "That's Taz," Scott said, pointing to a girl holding a guitar. "Jamie is on drums."

"Hey," Jamie said with a wave.

"Kylie plays keyboards, and Eddie is doing the recording," Scott finished as a guy in a red T-shirt waved from behind a glass wall. "Guys, this is Lizzie and Miranda."

Lizzie waved. "Hey."

"We're really glad you're here," Todd said warmly. "Scott showed us some of your lyrics—they're awesome. I have a few ideas about chord progressions. . . ."

"Showed you our lyrics?" Lizzie muttered, but she didn't have time to wonder where Scott had gotten them, because Taz was already picking out a few chords, and Lizzie had to hum the melody for her.

Lizzie, Miranda, and the band spent an hour or so nailing the music until Eddie thought they were ready to record.

"Which song should we start with?" Lizzie asked her best friend.

"Let's do the new one," Miranda suggested.

"Okay, everybody," Lizzie announced. "We're going to record 'True.'"

Eddie gave the "ready" signal, and Taz played the first few bars of the song. After a moment, the drums picked up the beat, then the rest of the band joined the melody.

Lizzie leaned toward her microphone. *This is my moment,* she thought. *Mine and Miranda's. We've got to make it count.* "'I've been chasing dreams for too long,'" Lizzie sang.

Miranda closed her eyes, as she belted,

"'Everything right seemed to turn out wrong . . .'"

Lizzie's voice rang clearly through the studio as she warmed to the familiar music. "'Just when I thought I'd reached the end, I realized all I needed . . .'"

"'Yes all I needed,'" Miranda sang.

Lizzie slipped her hand into Miranda's as she and her best friend blended their voices in harmony. "'Was one true friend. . . .'"

Once the song was over, the studio was completely silent for a moment. And then, suddenly, everyone was cheering and clapping. Scott let out a whoop.

"Guys, that was amazing!" Todd cried.

"We did it!" Miranda cheered, wrapping Lizzie into a huge hug.

"Okay, I'm going to listen to how it sounds," Eddie said over the speakers. "But I think we got it. Take a few minutes, everybody, then we can come back and do the next song."

Scott walked up to them. "Hey! That was great, you guys."

"Thanks," Lizzie said warmly.

"Listen, uh, I have to take off in a few minutes. So, uh, Miranda . . . can I . . . talk to you for a minute?" Scott asked.

Miranda shrugged. "Sure."

Scott's eyes flicked to Lizzie, and she got the hint. He wanted to talk to Miranda *alone.* "Oh, uh—yeah," Lizzie said quickly. "Well, I wanted to go over something with Taz, anyway."

Miranda nodded. "Okay."

He's going to ask her out, Lizzie thought giddily as she went and stood by the rest of the band. Scott's going to ask out Miranda! I've got to hear this. She tried to be sly as she made her way—half crouching—toward the drum set. She peered around to make sure that nobody was looking before she ducked behind the drums, just far enough away so that she wasn't obvious, but not too far . . .

"So," Scott was saying, "I heard what happened with Blaine. I'm really sorry."

"It's not like it was your fault," Miranda told him.

"Actually," Scott said, wincing, "it kind of was."

Lizzie froze. *What's he talking about?* she wondered.

Miranda looked as though Scott had just told her that he was from the planet Klometron. "What?" she asked. "How?"

"Well . . . actually," Scott said, "Blaine is my cousin."

"Oh," Miranda said, tucking her dark hair behind her ear. "But, well, that isn't your fault. We all have jerky relatives. I mean, last year, my uncle Hector ate a slice of my grandmother's birthday cake before she even blew out the candles!"

"No." Scott anxiously bit his lip. "No, I mean, this is different . . ." He cleared his throat. Then he seemed to switch the topic. "You know, I really like the Chocolate Rabbits."

"The Chocolate Rabbits?" Miranda repeated. "You mean the band? How do you know about them?"

"You told me," Scott said.

Miranda thought for a moment. "I did? When?"

"Online," Scott explained. "Chilipeppa17, I'm Waterboy335."

"What?" Miranda's voice was a strangled whisper.

Omigosh, Lizzie thought as she peered at Scott and Miranda from behind the cymbals on the drum set. That makes so much sense! That's how Todd knew about our lyrics—Miranda had sent their songs to Internet boy. And of course, the sweet, cool online guy had to be someone like Scott . . . but then, how did Blaine get into the picture? Or, more important, how did Blaine's picture get sent to Miranda?

"I'm the one you've been talking to," Scott explained. "And when you sent me your picture, I couldn't believe that you were the same cool girl that I already knew from the pool. . . ."

"So you sent Blaine to meet me?" Miranda sounded pretty skeptical.

Scott sighed and dug his hands into the pockets of his jeans. "I know it sounds stupid, but I thought that if you knew what I looked like, you wouldn't want to meet me. I mean, you're so pretty. . . ."

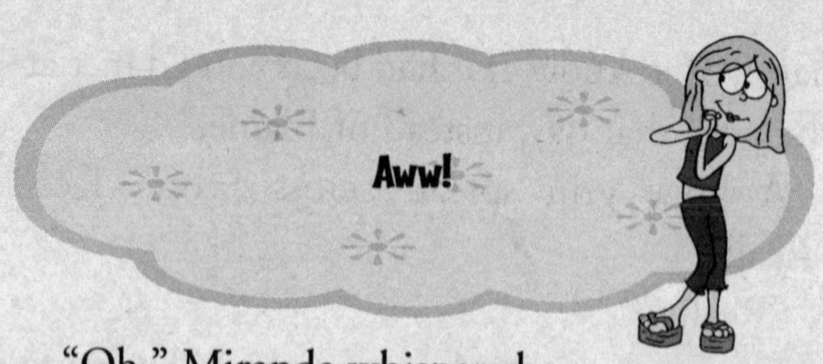

"Oh," Miranda whispered.

"So I sent you a photo of my older cousin, Blaine," Scott admitted. "But then I realized what a dumb idea that was. So I asked to meet you. And I *was* going to meet you in person, and tell you the whole truth—" He sounded really embarrassed as he added, "but then I chickened out at the last minute, and I asked Blaine to meet you, instead."

"You know, I really wish you hadn't done that," Miranda told him.

"I know," Scott admitted. "It was really stupid, and you probably hate me now—"

"No, it's not that," Miranda cut him off. "It's just that—I would have been really happy. You know, if it had been you I'd met at the pool that day, instead of Blaine."

A huge grin spread across Scott's face. "Really?"

"Really."

Omigosh, omigosh, omigosh! Is he going to kiss her? Lizzie thought frantically as she leaned forward to get a better look. What's happening? I can't see—these dumb cymbals are in my—

"Whoa—whoa!" Lizzie cried suddenly, as she lost her balance and fell headfirst into the drum set.

Crash!

By the time she managed to disentangle herself from the drums, Miranda was grinning from ear to ear . . . and so was Scott.

"So it's a date, then?" Scott asked as Lizzie dusted herself off.

"I'm cool," Lizzie said to the band members, who were gaping at her in confusion.

Miranda hadn't even noticed the crash—she was too busy gazing up at Scott. She nodded, blushing. "I'll see you then." She looked over at Lizzie, who gave her a thumbs-up.

So, Mister Right Guy really had shown up, after all, thought Lizzie happily.

"Okay, everybody," Eddie announced. "The first track sounds perfect. Let's work on the next song."

Could this day get any better? Lizzie thought as she took her place by the microphone.

"Which song do you want to do next?" Eddie asked.

Lizzie grinned at Miranda, who grinned back.

"I think it's time to do 'You Go, Girl,'" Lizzie said.

Miranda nodded. "Jamtacular."

CHAPTER THIRTEEN

"Out of the way, out of the way!" Miranda said as she rushed up Lizzie's front walk.

"Whoa, what's the rush?" Gordo asked.

"Today is the day that KZAP is supposed to let everyone know who won," Lizzie explained as she turned her key in the lock.

"Yeah, *some* people are still waiting to find out if they won their contests," Miranda pointed out as she pushed through Lizzie's door. "Unlike you, Gordo."

Lizzie laughed. Gordo had just found out that his film was going to be entered in a regional film festival. Lucy's had gotten Honorable Mention. It was a big deal, apparently.

"And we're kind of eager to get our prize," Miranda said, "since *no one* could have beaten our slammin' CD."

"Too true," Lizzie agreed. She had worked her backside off at the pool all summer, but it had been worth it. "Scott's brother and his friends did an excellent job with the backups." The CD sounded professional, and she and Miranda had been psyched to send it in.

"Okay, okay," Gordo said as Miranda dropped to the floor to sort through the mail, which had been shoved through the slot in the front door. "But just let me remind you that interfering with the mail is a federal offense."

Rolling her eyes, Miranda picked up the pile of mail and handed it to Lizzie.

"Bill, bill, bill," Lizzie said as she sifted through the pile of envelopes. "Card from Gammy McGuire, catalog, bill . . . *big, legal-size envelope from KZAP*!"

Miranda let out a squeal and started jumping up and down as Lizzie tore open the envelope.

" '*Dear Ms. McGuire and Ms. Sanchez,*' " she read aloud, " '*we are pleased to announce that you have been selected as one of the runners-up in our songwriting contest. . . .*' "

"Runner-up?" Miranda looked crushed.

"We . . . lost," Lizzie said. It took a moment for the news to sink in. I endured Tudgeman's minty breath, I dug up dandelions, I sweated and worked my butt off to get real studio time . . . and we didn't even get the record deal.

"I can't believe it." Miranda looked like she might start crying.

"What's going on in here?" Mrs. McGuire asked as she and her husband walked into the front hall.

"The KZAP contest," Lizzie said as she handed her mother the letter. "We didn't win."

"Aw, honey." Mrs. McGuire scanned the letter, and her forehead creased in confusion. "But it says here that they're going to play your song on KZAP's morning show. That's wonderful!"

"You girls worked really hard, and we're very proud of you both," Lizzie's dad told them.

"Thanks, Mr. McGuire," Miranda said as she gave Lizzie's shoulder a squeeze.

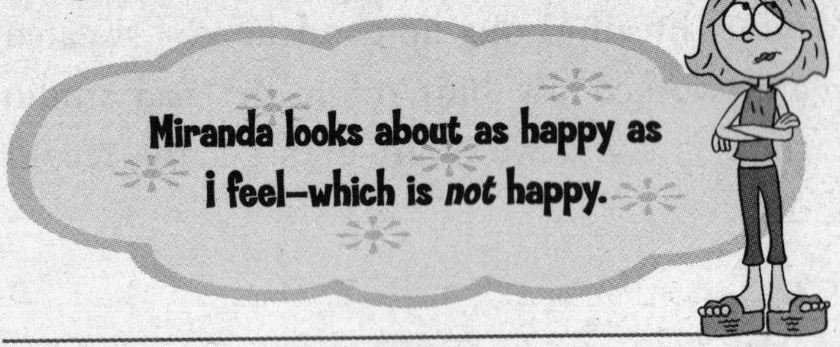

Miranda looks about as happy as i feel–which is *not* happy.

Mrs. McGuire wrapped her daughter in a hug. "You didn't lose," she said.

"That right," Mr. McGuire agreed, "there were professional songwriters and musicians in this contest. And you girls were right up there with the best of them. I think that calls for a celebration. How about some ice cream?"

Lizzie tried to force a smile, but she just couldn't do it. "I'm not sure I feel like it, Dad," Lizzie said.

"Hey," Gordo said suddenly. "You know that film festival my documentary is in? There are going to be tons of entertainment types there."

Lizzie and Miranda glared at him.

How can Gordo be so smart and so clueless at the same time?

"Way to rub salt in the wound, Gordo," Miranda snapped.

"No, no—you don't get it," Gordo said. "What I'm saying is—maybe your song 'Fakers' could be the soundtrack to my movie. It totally works with the theme. And I was thinking the film needed something, anyway."

Lizzie's eyes widened. "And then maybe some producers would hear it. . . ."

Gordo nodded. "Besides, remember Tucker Felix?"

Lizzie nodded. "The DJ from Shango Tango."

"Right. Apparently the polka I brought in was such a huge hit, she wants me to keep an ear out for any other hot new beats." Gordo shrugged. "She said she'd spin anything I brought in."

"Omigosh!" Miranda cried. "That's amazing, Gordo! Everyone goes there!"

it's nice to have friends who've got your back.

"And look—your song is going to be on KZAP's morning show. Everyone wakes up to that show. Don't worry," Gordo told them, "you'll have a record deal in no time."

"Then this really does call for ice cream," Mr. McGuire announced, jingling his car keys.

"I'm there," Gordo said.

"Okay, Gordo," Miranda said as she walked with him to the McGuires' car, "we're going to need a credit at the end of your film. . . ."

Mrs. McGuire placed a hand on her daughter's shoulder. "I'm proud of you, honey."

Lizzie looked up at her mom. "For what?"

"For working so hard to make your dream come true," Mrs. McGuire said sincerely. "And for not giving up, even when things didn't turn out the way you expected."

Lizzie thought about that for a moment. True, the junior lifeguarding class hadn't been what she thought it would be. Neither had her job at the pool. And not winning the KZAP contest had definitely been a disappointment. But things worked out great anyway, Lizzie realized, for all of them.

After all, she thought as she and her mom walked toward the car, with friends like mine, how could I ever really lose?

"What's up, guys?" Gordo asked as Matt and Lanny walked into the kitchen. Gordo pulled another slice of pizza from the box in front of Miranda. After ice cream, Lizzie's friends had decided to stay over for dinner.

"Yeah," Miranda chimed in, "where are all of your hairstyle groupies?"

Lanny and Matt exchanged looks.

"Do you know the problem with hair?" Matt demanded.

"Um, do you mean yours specifically?" Lizzie asked. "Because I can think of about a hundred problems. Starting with the fact that 'porcupine' is not a fashion statement."

"The problem with hair," Matt said, ignoring his sister, "is that it keeps on growing! Haircuts, haircuts—everyone needs haircuts!" He yanked on his own prickly mop, eyes wide. "By the way, Gordo, you need a haircut." Matt snapped his fingers and Lanny flipped through a large black notebook. "I can fit you in on—"

"No, no," Gordo said quickly. "That's okay, Matt. I think I'm good."

"But your hair is flopping in your face again," Matt protested.

A smile crept up the side of Gordo's face. "I think I kind of like it this way."

"Hey, Gordo, by the way, whatever happened to your stylin' wardrobe?" Lizzie asked. He was back in his old uniform—vintage shirt over concert T-shirt and cargo pants.

"Gave it away to the Salvation Army," Gordo announced.

"So, no more cool, Gordo?" Miranda asked.

"From now on, I'm keeping all of my cool where it counts," Gordo declared. "On the inside."

Matt sighed as he collapsed into a chair at the table. "I wish other people felt that way. All of these haircuts are driving me crazy. I don't want to do it anymore. I mean, Lanny and I have saved enough money to build our rocket—but now we don't even have enough time to do it."

Lanny nodded miserably.

"I'm a prisoner of my own talent!" Matt wailed.

"Well—you could give someone a lousy haircut," Gordo suggested. "Then word would get around, and nobody would want you to cut their hair anymore. They'd say you lost your magic touch."

Matt thought for a moment. "But most of the people whose hair I cut are my friends . . ." he said. "I wouldn't want to give any of them a bad haircut."

Just then, there was a wild tapping on the French doors, and a moment later, Kate Sanders slid them open and walked into the kitchen, completely ignoring Lizzie and her friends.

"Matt McGuire," Kate snapped, "I need a haircut."

"Oh. Well, sorry. You have to make an appointment—" Matt started to say politely, but Kate rudely cut him off.

"Are you crazy? I'm not making an appointment." Kate glared at Lanny, who had just flipped open his notebook. "I need a haircut *now.*"

"Hey, lay off my brother, Kate," Lizzie warned.

Okay, so i don't usually leap to Matt's defense. But *nobody* bosses my little bro around—except me, of course. Especially not Kate.

"You can't just come in here and bully him—" Lizzie continued, but Matt waved his hands.

"No, Lizzie," he said, jumping to his feet.

"Actually, it's okay." Then he turned to the Queen of Mean. "I'll cut your hair, Kate."

"Matt, you don't have to," Lizzie told him.

"Yes, he does," Kate snapped.

"It's all right," Matt said. "I think I'll take Gordo's advice and handle one more customer today."

Gordo's advice? Lizzie repeated to herself. She glanced at Miranda, who was choking back a giggle. Suddenly, Lizzie got it. A grin broke out over her face.

"Oh, yeah," said Lizzie. "Gordo's advice. . . ."

"So, Kate," said Matt, "are you ready to step into my office?"

"Just make it quick," Kate griped as she followed Matt and Lanny upstairs. "I have to be at my dad's country club in an hour and a half."

"Oh, it'll be over before you know it," Matt promised. "And then my career as a stylist extraordinaire will finally be over, too," he murmured under his breath. "Thank goodness."

"I am not responsible for this," Gordo whispered once Kate was out of earshot.

Lizzie and Miranda dissolved into giggles.

"So!" Lizzie said brightly. "What are we up to tonight?"

"Scott and I are going to the park. They're showing *The Wizard of Oz* on a giant screen," Miranda said. "Want to come with?"

"Sure," Lizzie said. "Gordo?"

"I'm in," Gordo promised. "Okay if I invite Lucy?"

"Definitely," Lizzie said. Lucy was really nice, and Lizzie was glad that she and Gordo had become buddies.

In the end, Lizzie knew the summer hadn't really gone the way she or her friends had expected. But, even though it had seemed kind of out of control at times, they still ended up with one slammin' CD, an excellent movie, and two cool new friends.

As summers go, i'd call that a sizzling success.